McGowan's Call

Also by Rob Smith:

Night Voices
Children of Light
The Spell of Twelve

Rob Smith

McGowan's Call

Drinian Press/
Huron, Ohio

McGowan's Call

Visit us online at www.DrinianPress.com.

.

This is a work of fiction. Names characters, places, and events are either the product of the author's mind or are used fictitiously. Any resemblance to actual persons, living or dead, businesses, events, or locales is entirely coincidental.

Cover design by Drinian Press.

Library of Congress Control Number: 2007904109

ISBN-10: 0-9785165-5-9
ISBN-13: 978-0-9785165-5-0

DrinianPress.com
Printed in the United States

Rob Smith

McGowan's Call

Contents:

Hatteras

While the rules of life in small towns vary from region to region, there is a universal regulation that *locals* are prohibited from telling the *imports* where the land mines of public opinion are buried. In Hatteras, an import is defined as any person not legally installed as a resident within forty-eight hours of birth. The forty-eight hour rule was instituted as a concession to the fact that there is no hospital within the city limits. Everyone suspects that those fortunate enough to be born at home are the real locals.

Davis McGowan had served as pastor in a number of small towns before landing in Hatteras, Ohio. He was aware that being liked was as good as it could get in a place where he would never really belong. The city was built on a high bank of the Ohio River and had withstood the ravages of flooding and, as some would tell it, the flow of pastors through the manse of the Presbyterian Church. Tonight he was less concerned with his social status than the weather forecast. The report called for the season's first Arctic Clipper which would drop down from Canada and bring sub-zero temperatures.

"Beth," he called to his wife, "do you have any real attachment to that old Boy Scout sleeping bag that you used to take to camp?"

"Not really," she answered. "What do you want it for?"

"It's supposed to get really cold tonight, and…"

"You're worried about Brodie," she said, cutting him off. "How are you going to get him to take it?"

"I thought I'd put the trash out early," he answered.

"It is nearly the Brodie-hour," she observed.

Brodie was one of the features of Hatteras. The locals all knew his story and advised walking a wide circle around him. Still, many were moved to pity for this homeless man whose paranoia made him lash out against those who offered even a kindly gesture.

Like most people, Brodie was a creature of habit. At dusk, he would walk through the alley that ran behind the church and the manse where the McGowans made their home. He cut a strange silhouette in his daily pilgrimage to find an unlocked door or wind-sheltered corner near some abandoned shop. For a while, open doors were common enough, but the old Francy Building was being renovated into apartments and the new owner was meticulous about security. Brodie was severely bent over and walked like a miser scanning the ground for wayward pennies. His long arms extended behind his back as a counter-balance. Dogs usually bounded along with him. Rumor had it that they were his sleeping partners on cold nights, dozing in a heap like litter mates warding off the cold weather.

2

When Davis first came to Hatteras, the vision of Brodie and his dog pack took him by surprise. His local tour guide seemed hardly to notice, but a comment by McGowan became an invitation to a longer conversation. "Did he have an accident that caused a spinal injury?" he had asked.

"Oh, that's Brodie," came the answer, "he's always walked like that. I doubt if any doctor could ever make a diagnosis. He'd bite their head off if they tried to get close."

The frank observation did not do much to quell initial fears when the McGowans took up residence in the church manse. It was not long before Beth and Davis discovered that their new home was located on Brodie's alley of opportunity. The pickings in the trash cans behind the church were a real bonanza after church suppers and the annual rummage sales.

Initially, they heeded local advice and cleared out of the alley before Brodie's nightly vigil. On one occasion, however, Davis startled Brodie and himself when he rounded the corner of the yellow brick building.

"Oh, sorry," was Davis' quick response.

"Reverend," said the gruff old man.

That was the extent of the conversation, but it moved McGowan. It totally flew in the face of all his assumptions. Everyone spoke of Brodie as a walking shape that was oblivious to his surroundings. With one word, Brodie proved that to be a lie. The McGowans were *imports* who could be mostly ignored by those outside his Presbyterian flock. Yet, this anti-social, paranoid vagrant somehow knew him, at least from a distance.

For a moment the two stood frozen in time. Brodie was first to break the spell. His bent form scooped up a wayward pop can and flung it into the gaping cavern of the church dumpster. It struck Davis that he was cleaning the trash out of the alley.

"Thank you," he said, mostly from habit. Brodie cocked his head to one side, looking like an outtake from the *Hunchback of Notre Dame*. He gave a grimace that was as close to a smile as he had probably managed in years.

Later that week, Davis was having coffee with the funeral director from across the street. "Tell me about Brodie," he asked.

"What's to tell? He's crazy!"

"But was he always?"

After a long silence and a sip of coffee, Brodie's story began, "My father told me about him. Not many people know this, but his given name is *Cecil*. My dad said that if you ever called him that, he'd just swear a blue-streak at you and walk away. He was always a loner, but he worked for years at the clay plant before it closed down. He did piece work mostly. He'd get paid by the number of clay pipes he could mould each shift. Evidently he worked fast, and his stuff never fell apart when they were fired in the kiln.

"Dad knew this because he had worked at the pottery while he saved up the money to go to mortuary school. He said that the plant manager would always offer to help Brodie with his finances. He'd ask Brodie if he was putting aside any money, and he'd be willing to go to the bank with him."

"What did Brodie say?"

"Only that it was his money and he didn't trust banks! Anyway, plastic pipe came along and all the clay works shut down. By then Brodie was pretty old, stubborn, and mean as hell."

"What about Social Security?" asked Davis.

"You'd have to ask Brodie on that one," came the reply. "Good luck! He's so old that I'd guess that he never applied for a number and never filed a tax form."

Davis' thoughts came back to Brodie for days after that conversation. He remembered his internship at the state mental hospital while he was a seminary student at Princeton. (Hatteras was a long way from Princeton.) He had spent time with patients whose personal stories could stand along side of Brodie's. He remembered an African-American woman who told him about her one living relative, an uncle who gave her "love and affection." It was an awakening for McGowan when his field-work supervisor told him that, in this case, "love and affection" was a euphemism for sexual abuse. She was institutionalized because she had nowhere else to go. He recalled the dismal conditions of the locked wards inhabited with drugged-out zombies. Those places were all closed now. It was not that mental illness was better treated, it was that warehousing was replaced with the idea that these people could fend for themselves on the streets.

In the old days, thought Davis, Brodie would have been one of those men who threw a brick through a window when the weather turned sour. After being arrested, he would have been confined to the state hospital for observation. In spring, when the weather turned warm, he would wander off from the hospital and, like the swallows returning to Capistrano, appear again on the streets of Hatteras. That game was no longer being played.

Davis found the faded pea-green sleeping bag on a shelf in the basement. He unrolled it and emptied the change from his pocket. He had $1.47 in coin. He dumped the coins into the bag and shook them down to the bottom. Brodie accepted no charity, so this had to look like the money that would roll out of the jeans of a sleeping scout.

When he came upstairs to the kitchen, Beth was busy at the counter crushing cheerios, peanuts, and raisins in a plastic bag. "What are you doing?" asked McGowan.

"Making some well-worn trail-mix, of course."

Davis smiled. "Looking after Brodie is becoming a team sport." He stuffed the food bag into a curl of the tightly rolled pack.

The night air took his breath when he walked out the back door and headed for the shadowy alley. "That arctic front hasn't even hit yet," he thought as the shivers raised goose bumps on his whole body. He propped the canvas bundle on top of a full can. He had made it just in time. From not too far away, he could hear the yelping of dogs and knew that Brodie would soon turn into the lane. He hurried back toward the warmth of the kitchen. "Still," he thought, "Brodie is mentally ill, but not stupid."

Come spring, Davis would find the bag rolled up on the back porch like a library book returned after hours. It was not, after all, charity. It was a game of mutual respect between a local and an import.

The Wake

Davis McGowan moved quickly to silence the ringing phone. The baby was finally quiet after a long night of crying, and in spite of the fact that it was after 10:00 a.m. on a Saturday morning, it was too early!

"Hello. Yes, Lucille. No, I haven't seen the news. One of your boarders, you say. William McKendry? That's fine. I never charge for a funeral, you said the right thing. I'll call Mark at the funeral home. Are you okay? Is someone with you right now? Good, I'll take care of it right away." He hung up the phone.

"Was that Lucille Caulder?" asked Beth, rolling over in bed.

"Yes," answered Davis, "apparently there's been some sort of accident this morning. One of the old men who rents a room from her was hit by a train. It's already been picked up by the local news."

"That's awful," said Beth sitting up, alert.

"His name was William McKendry. His habit was to go uptown for coffee every morning. Evidently, today he was on his way back when he got hit crossing the tracks."

"Do you know him?" she asked.

"No. Lucille said he was ninety-two and pretty much kept to himself. His only outings were daily coffee with a dwindling group of other old timers. No family as far as she knows."

"Poor Lucille, she probably feels like she has to take care of everything."

"That's what she called about. She told Mark Brunner at the funeral home that he could call me about services. Afterward, she thought that maybe I wouldn't do a funeral for a stranger."

"I never knew you to turn away a family in crisis."

"I wouldn't want to," answered Davis. "She said that he didn't have any money and how much would I charge, his not being a church member and all."

"She's a sweetie," said Beth warmly.

"You heard me say that I wouldn't charge anything and that I'd take care of it. Her daughter came down from Piney to sit with her."

"Are you going to call Mark then?"

"I suspect that he's not in the office right now with all this going on, but I'll leave a message with Ruth saying I'll do the service gratis."

The phone call to the Brunner Funeral Home lasted only a few minutes. Davis had guessed rightly that Mark would not be there. Evidently, he was with a sheriff's deputy going through McKendry's room looking for anything which could identify the next of kin. The man was ninety-two, and while Mark's father had provided services for the man's wife fifteen years earlier, all the

9

names on the old list of her surviving family members had already been transferred to Hilltop Cemetery.

Brunner didn't return his call that day, but McGowan didn't worry. He would see Mark at the normal rendezvous at the local greasy spoon for coffee. The town still ran, or at least pretended to run, on the old-boy network. The insurance offices, the savings and loan, and the funeral director followed the daily practice of unlocking the front doors of their offices, making sure the office staff was set for the day, and then they headed off for morning coffee. Occasionally, morning coffee took all morning. The fact that Davis was included in the group was a real coup. It meant that the movers and shakers appreciated his banter. He had to wonder, however, if it was all an illusion. The offices of these men apparently functioned quite well without them, but that thought was not as disconcerting in Hatteras as it was in the corporate world.

The group never gossiped, at least not according to local definitions. "Women gossip," they would insist, "men just share information."

It was an old adage, but McGowan learned early on that a small amount of corrective information, placed in the appropriate ear, could stifle some of the cruelty of the small town grapevine. Most of the time in the group was spent in insider jokes and the prospects of the two local teams, the Hatteras Harriers and the Pittsburgh Steelers. If juicy gossip was exchanged, it was usually after the group had disbanded and during the trek back to the offices.

McGowan's Call

It was natural that the death of William McKendry would come up at coffee. McGowan knew little of the details, and he was pleased when Mark Brunner stuck fairly close to the account that was in the morning paper. The details were sketchy. A ninety-two year old man, legally blind with coke-bottle glasses had walked (or stumbled) into the side of a moving train at the Main Street crossing. Funeral services were scheduled for 10:00 a.m. at the Brunner Funeral Home, Rev. Davis McGowan officiating.

When the *new information* only affirmed what was already known, the subject shifted to the time a gondola car had jumped the track dumping fifteen tons of corn in the alley behind the shops. Eye contact between Brunner and McGowan said that there were other details, but this was not the time or place.

The funeral home was directly across the street from the Presbyterian Church. So when the procession from the coffee shop dwindled to two, Davis and Mark were speaking in private.

"McKendry's wife died ten or fifteen years ago," said Brunner, "ever since, he's kept to himself. Lived in a room and took most of his meals with Lucille. She has a few old men that she sort of takes care of. They'd probably be living on the street if she didn't take them in. Anyway, he'd go down to Snake's every morning for coffee."

"I thought Snake's was just a bar where you couldn't be admitted if you had all your own teeth," said

McGowan, in a tone that carried over from the coffee group.

"Well, that's after the second shift lets out at the mill," explained Brunner. "In the morning, Snake puts on coffee and a few old guys come in when the all-nighters are sobering up (or at least getting as sober as they ever do).

"Anyway, the old guys are getting fewer and fewer and yesterday, McKendry took a walk into the side of a train."

"The paper implied that it was an accident," offered McGowan. "He was legally blind, wasn't he?"

"Yes, according to Lucille, he really could only see light and dark shadows. The police don't know. Even if you don't see a train, you feel it when it's getting close."

Davis nodded. He had to agree. Trains ran through Hatteras like it wasn't there and the rumble of the ground announced their arrival before the crossing gates flashed red.

"He was old and alone," continued Brunner, his voice trailed off. Both were silent until they reached the alley entrance of the funeral parlor. Mark indicated that Davis should follow him in. The two made their way through the parking bays of the garage and into the small room that passed for an employee lounge. McGowan sensed that there was more that Brunner wanted or needed to say about a troubling death.

Without prompting, Mark picked up where he had left off. "When the paper hit the street, we began getting phone calls. People wanted to help. Jenks said he had an old suit that still looked good that we could bury him in. Bob Williams, from your church, called to volunteer to be a pallbearer. He had been one when McKendry's wife died however-many years ago and figured that there would not be many people around who would remember him."

"That's pretty nice," offered McGowan. "Did he have any family at all?"

"Yes, we tracked down a nephew and a niece up in East Lisbon, but they don't give a damn."

"What?"

"We called them when we found their number in his room. They said they really hadn't seen him in years and that he hadn't been much of an uncle anyway. They're not planning to come down or anything. They're probably afraid that they might get stuck with a bill."

"That wouldn't happen, would it?"

"No, he was a vet and there are some places we could tap to give him a modest burial."

"So William McKendry is going to be buried in a borrowed suit, and he didn't live to experience his fifteen minutes of fame that came from the press release."

"You'd think so," commented Brunner. "Right after we talked to his niece and nephew we found a savings passbook. When the cops checked with the bank, we found that he had more than twenty four thousand dollars stashed away."

"Whoa!" said McGowan.

"Exactly."

"Where is that going?" asked Davis.

"With no will, to his nearest relatives," offered Mark, "but hell if he's going to be buried in a borrowed suit and packed in a cloth-covered casket. When they find out, I hope they feel real guilty about getting the cash."

"Will they?"

"No, they'll probably yell about why I wasn't smart enough to use a borrowed suit. I feel sorry for the old guy."

Davis left the funeral home by the front door and crossed against the light to the alley that led to the church office. Most of the time, traffic lights on Main Street weren't necessary. The exception was Friday nights when the Harriers took the field.

As he worked on the funeral service, he was well aware that he would be mostly speaking to an empty room. No one would blame him if he simply read the Twenty-third Psalm and offered a standard prayer, but William McKendry asked more questions in his dying breath than many in an entire lifetime.

Was his death an accident or a statement? Had he had enough, and did not want to be the last of his generation? Why did he live on the edge of poverty when he had enough to bring, at least, some comfort? Where did the money come from? What was he saving his money for? Was it the proceeds of his wife's insurance? That would be money he would never touch because it came at too high a price. In a cloud of confusion, did he forget that it was there? When his wife died, he had friends; why did he shun them? Was his grief so over powering that he avoided them as the living reminders of his loss and happier days?

Davis knew that he would find no answers in the swirl of conjecture that now filled his brain. He didn't need any answers. Those would be the fodder of the gossip mongers. He stuck with what he knew. William McKendry was a man who once lived, who once loved, and who now was beyond the things that his money could have bought, but that his heart rejected.

He chose a simple passage from Matthew: *Two sparrows are bought for a penny, and if one of them falls to the ground, your Father knows. Even the hairs on your head are numbered. Do not be afraid, you matter more than many sparrows.* He had been reading the text in the Greek, but he knew his translation would not differ much from the Bible that he would carry to the service.

He was right about the crowd. When he entered the funeral home, Mark Brunner took him to one side. "Would you be willing to be a pallbearer? There won't be enough people here to handle the casket."

"Sure," said McGowan. "How about the family?"

"Are you kidding? They couldn't be bothered. But Old Bill looks good, I'm sending him out in style."

"Mark, they'll nail you for running up the costs!"

"Maybe, but I've already decided to slide my profit on this one to Lucille. She's taken care of him, and there are a couple more staying at her place. I figure it's just a fairer way to leave something for his real family."

Davis couldn't argue.

15

The service was short, but not of the cookie-cutter variety. Brunner had arranged a family limo for Lucille, Bob Williams, and a younger man that Davis couldn't identify. Lucille protested at first, but smiled through teary eyes when Mark insisted that it was all a part of the service.

Williams, the younger man, Brunner, and Davis struggled to lift the heavy oak casket into the hearse. McGowan wondered how the four would handle the longer trek at the cemetery.

"Slim and the caretaker will help at the cemetery," said Mark, anticipating the question. His word was true. When the four approached the coach at the cemetery, they were joined by two others. Davis recognized the tall lanky form of Slim, the foreman from the vault company that he saw on every funeral from Brunner Funeral Home. Slim wore his familiar coveralls, and next to him was an older man in jeans and a red flannel shirt. There were now six to bear the weight up a gentle rise and place it squarely over two planks set across the open grave. After a short prayer, Lucille went back to the car. Davis had done enough funerals to know the drill.

"Reverend, did Markey give you that old story about his weak back?" bantered Slim. It was an old gag by now, and Davis smiled at the good-natured man.

"Yep," said McGowan, "told me that he was under doctor's orders not to do any lifting."

Slim passed the heavy woven straps under the casket at each end. He took one end of a strap in his hand.

16

Davis took the strap on the opposite side while Brunner and the younger man handled the second strap.

"Gentlemen, if you'd just take up the slack and lift on my word," said Slim. "Okay, lift!"

The casket came up off the planks and the cemetery worker slid the heavy boards back away from the hole.

"Now, let out the slack," said Slim. Slowly the box was lowered and the four men fed the excess strap through their grip. When the weight came to rest in the concrete vault, the lines went slack. McGowan looked at Bob Williams who had stood watching.

"I hope he's at rest now," said Williams to no one.

"Thank you, Gentlemen," said Slim. "I can take it from here." He was already moving toward the wheeled caddy that would help him position the concrete lid to seal the vault. It was something he had done a thousand times, maybe a million.

"I never met him." McGowan looked up to see that the youngest pallbearer had stepped up beside him.

"What?" he asked.

"Mr. McKendry," said the man. "I didn't know him. I read about it in the paper. He was Irish and I'm Irish, too. I figure that no Irishman should be buried without a wake of some sort, so I'm planning to go out and get drunk!" With that, the man stepped back toward the waiting limo. Davis was hit with a stunned silence.

"Who is the younger guy?" he finally said to Brunner.

"You mean Fitzpatrick?"

"I guess. The other pallbearer."

17

"That's Danny Fitzpatrick. Spends most of his time drinking himself to an early grave."

"He says that he's going to get drunk tonight to honor McKendry."

"Never knew him to need an excuse before," added Brunner.

"He may have never needed one, but he has one tonight."

House Across the Road

Back in the late sixties there was a folk song that had the line, "Jesus was a sailor when he walked upon the water." I don't know if it was technically correct, but according to Matthew's Gospel, he knew about "red sky at night."

I always understood "Red sky at night, sailor's delight" as an omen of good weather. I remember, however, one occasion when there was a noticeable color shift, and the red became an eerie orange/pink combination. If you've ever seen it, you'd know the color.

It was in early spring, and I had a rare Friday evening wedding. It was nothing fancy. They were an older couple; it was a second marriage for both of them. The service was to be just a few friends; one of them was to bring his camera to take some pictures.

A line of violent thunderstorms had passed through, and then the orange/pink. The phone rang at the church. It was the photographer friend explaining that he couldn't get through. The road was blocked and there were no quick alternate routes.

"There's a house across the road," he said. "Traffic can't get through." The ceremony took place as

19

scheduled and afterwards, I remember that I took some pictures of the couple using the bride's camera.

I was locking up the church when the phone rang again. The hospital had been trying to reach me. Tornados had ripped through a valley, and the injured were being taken to the area emergency rooms. Since I was on the disaster response team, they asked me to come and deal with families looking for their loved ones. They briefed me when I arrived at the auditorium that had been dubbed the "staging area." As it turned out, the room was much larger than needed. No families had arrived, but they had reports of a dozen or so with injuries transported to four hospitals. With no communication networks, they thought families would be roaming between hospitals trying to find those whisked off in ambulances. One young woman had been sent by ambulance to Pittsburgh. That long trip was risky, but the choppers were all grounded and her injuries too severe for the local medical centers.

At this hospital they had a Jane Doe in surgery. They had no name or identification. She was alive in spite of the fact that a two-by-four had lodged in her neck. Miraculously, no major blood vessels or nerves were severed.

When the staff left, I sat alone in the cavernous room. Forty-five minutes later, four people straggled in. They were a little younger than I. They were two men and two women in their twenties. The volunteer attendant at the information desk in the main lobby had directed them to the auditorium. They looked like the wandering dead.

This had been their second hospital. At the last, they had waited more than an hour to find that their mother was not there. I had more questions than answers:

"Were you with your mother when the storm hit? Do you know if she was hurt badly? Do you know what kind of injury she had? What was she wearing?"

My questions proved fruitless. They were miles away when the storm hit and drove to what was left of her home after the ambulance had cleared the area. Neighbors weren't sure what the medics had said, if anything. I called up to the surgical suite, and was updated.

"The reason I asked all these questions is that we have a patient in surgery right now. We don't know if it's your mother, but she's about the right age. Would one of you be willing to go into the surgery to identify her?"

They all nodded.

"I'll warn you that she won't look like herself. The Docs are doing a good job and all indications are that she will be alright, but there will be a lot of tubes and she's swollen up. That's a normal body response, but she'll look real bloated."

Glances passed between them, and one of the young men said, "I'll do it."

With that I led them to the elevators and we went to the surgical waiting area on the third floor. The nursing staff was at full complement, so I was dismissed to go back to the auditorium and my vigil. Later, I heard that Jane Doe was their mother and that she had pulled through. The descriptions of her injury, however, took years to shake off.

I never made it back to the auditorium.

"Reverend, they want you down at the emergency room" was my introduction to an impossible situation. I was to meet the man whose wife had been ambulanced to Pittsburgh. He was outside the emergency room waiting for news about his toddler daughter who was also being attended.

As we paced through the corridors, an orderly gave me the outline of the story. The husband had been working his shift at the steel plant. They lived in a trailer set up on a farm. Men had been working in the barn when the weather alert broke onto the regular TV broadcast. Seeing the warning, his wife ran outside to warn the men. She had just gotten back to her child in the mobile home when it took a direct hit. She and her two-year-old were the most critical victims of the storm. Medics thought that there might have been hope for her if they could get her to Allegheny General, but a helicopter was out of the question with storms still in the area. They had less hope for the child.

The husband/father was probably under twenty-five. He was pulled out of work and offered a sedative, which he took. His look was gaunt and he was weighed down with a fatigue reminiscent of the looks seen in photos shot through barbed wire in concentration camps. His expression did not change when word came back that his wife had not made it to Pittsburgh. I suspect that, at times such as these, the human body loses its capacity to express anything more through the numbness.

I was called down to help him deal with the fact that his daughter was also now dead in the next room. I held his hand as I led him into the small, tightly packed room. The medical staff parted like the Red Sea, even the machines wheeled away from the big bed which housed the tiny body.

The ER Doc kept glancing between the father and me as he explained what had been done. I realized that he was looking for a response, some expression of recognition. Seeing none in the father's face, he looked to me as if asking, "Am I saying anything that can be understood?"

His words were accurate, clinical, and true. At times I thought he was pleading for forgiveness for a crime that he had not committed. The little girl was beautiful and perfect in spite of the spinal fluid which drained from her left ear. She and her mother were now beyond worry and fear, but the young man who stood next to me was not.

Sometimes prayer seems like a little thing, but it is all that we had.

Family arrived and took the young widower home. It wasn't until the next day's newspaper came that I even learned his last name.

The truth is that the little girl looked like my young daughter, maybe like the daughter of every father on the planet. I wanted to hold my family close, and I wanted to erase the terrible images of what storms do to human bodies.

That weekend I suggested a trip to the boat. We could sail a few hours and let the wind perform its cosmic dance of healing rather than its swirling path of destruction. It was a bad idea.

The road to the lake steadily provided scenes of devastation. Giant trees were uprooted and saplings twisted like corkscrews. My woodcutting friends told me later that those twisted shoots became time-bombs. As the tree adds to its growth rings, it retains the energy of the storm. Years later, when a chainsaw is set to those trunks the tree will spring out and foil the cutter who tries to direct its fall. I don't know if that is true. If it is, I, at least, wanted to forget what the tree would remember.

There was some tree damage near the marina. I had hoped that this would be one place where the storm would not have left its mark. Even so, I suspected that the shoreline would heal more quickly than I.

The guy at the bait shop seemed truly disgusted that I would come to play on my boat when lives had been lost. I couldn't argue. It was on my mind, too.

Sister Mary

It was a simpler time. It was before anyone had thought of the Internet, much less the predators who have learned to reproduce themselves there. I was always looking for ways to help members of the congregation put a face on mission, but a cynical few always touted that it was just another excuse for taking more of their money. I wanted them to see that it was about making a difference.

Seated next to me at a United Way luncheon was Sister Mary Margaret. I knew her mostly by reputation. She directed Catholic Social Services and was known for her ability to get things done. I understood her effect on my Catholic friends, but not the Protestants. Most of my Catholic friends had her as a teacher in the fourth grade. She had been one of the nuns who taught at St. Christopher's school. Even now, if she called them by their given names, it was like they were in the fourth grade all over again and they had just been caught passing a note to the pretty girl in the third row. But she had the same affect on the Protestants, so I knew it wasn't *all* about childhood guilt.

As I sat through the planning meeting, I began to get a different picture of Sister Mary. She was organized, straightforward, and articulate. She had a clear vision of the "right thing to do" and assumed that everyone around her would want to participate in what was only fair and correct. I could see that if you didn't have a similar agenda in mind, it would be much safer to walk a wide circle around this determined woman.

After the meeting, I approached her with a question. "Sister," I said, "I need a project to help the Presbyterians understand that gifts of money become very down-to-earth help for real people. Is there anything in particular that you need for your summer day camp program? Maybe something that you can't cover with grant money or donations? You can think about it and get back to me."

Her mind worked faster than mine. She didn't have to think about it at all. "Underwear," she said.

"What?"

"Underwear," she repeated. "Poor kids don't wear any. The kids at camp come out of the projects. In the summer, they'd be home all alone and unsupervised, so we use local church buses and take them out to the 4-H camp. We provide them an activity, lunch, and a safe place. When it's really hot, they could play in the creek, but they don't have bathing suits. The little ones could swim in their undershorts, but they don't have any. Their families can get used clothes at garage sales and second hand stores, but you can't buy used underwear, so, they don't wear any."

Her bluntness took me by surprise. I'm not sure why, given what I had seen from her earlier. (Did I mention that this was a more innocent time when small children on a beach wearing underwear was not unusual or considered sexual?)

"I think that we could do something that will help," I said. "Give me a few days and I'll get back to you." It didn't take a few days; it only took a few phone calls. The special Lenten offerings would be directed to Catholic Services' summer camp program. A manager in a local retail store offered a 50% discount on the merchandise and we were off and running.

Within three weeks we had a mountain of tube socks, t-shirts, and underpants in a full range of children's sizes. I was surprised by the generosity of the people and after we maxed out the need, we sent along an additional check.

There was another price to pay for Sister Mary's idea, and I was the one to pay. It wasn't really a problem, but came in the form of unrelenting teasing. Church members never failed to point out that when I carried my visual aids into the sanctuary, I restricted myself to the tube socks and t-shirts. The deepest cut came from a friend who saddled up along side me and whispered, "I don't want to be the bearer of dirty gossip, but there's a rumor going around town that you are into Sister Mary Margaret's underwear."

Valentine's Gift

Visiting parishioners on the Alzheimer's wing of the nursing home was always an exercise in futility. It was not that the patients were difficult to deal with so much as it was that the whole reason for the visit had very little to do with the patient.

Davis McGowan knew exactly how and where he would find Mary Simons even before he got in his car to make the forty-five minute journey south of Dayton to the nursing home in Monroe. Unless her condition had changed, this visit would be just like his last, and like the one before that. She would be dressed in her flannel robe and seated in a chair by the nurses' station. As he approached her, she would look up and say, "I wondered when you would get here today."

Mary started every conversation that way. Davis knew that if he walked away for five minutes and came back, she'd give the same greeting. Their conversation would be pleasant and, for the most part, coherent. It just wouldn't be remembered. Therein lay the problem.

Visits to the Alzheimer's wing were not for the benefit of the patient, they were for the benefit of the family. Mary's children were now in their early sixties.

28

They, too, would hear the same greeting upon arrival and sense the same emptiness in their mother who was there, but not there. Still, they would return and have their hearts broken, yet again. Davis made these visits for them. He hoped that their finding his calling card by the bed would tell them that they were not the only ones who remembered their mother. It was a lot of responsibility to place on a piece of heavy paper that could easily find its way to the trash when the housekeeper came through. He thought of buying them a guestbook so that visitors could sign in. Why was it that he only thought of that when he was already at the home and not when he was at the mall where he could just buy a lousy guestbook? "Next time, I'll remember," he pledged as he entered 1-9-9-1 on the keypad that activated the electric doors that secured the wing.

He didn't have to ask for the code. Though the code was changed annually, he already knew what it was. Dementia patients can often recall the past, but hardly ever the present. The code was always the year.

As he walked through the portal, he could see Mary seated at her station. He would rue the day when she wasn't there. People called the disease Alzheimer, but most often people of Mary's age had some other form of dementia. They were all part of a class of illnesses that took their victims a little at a time and then found a plateau. Once it leveled off, it sometimes seemed like it would go on, unchanged forever. "Forever" was too big a word. Eventually Mary's cheerfulness would be gone as she slipped into the netherworld of losing her identity.

There was a bedridden stage, yet to come. It was this stage that was the ugliest, and families would find themselves praying for death and feeling guilty. In the past, pneumonia was the legacy of the bedridden. In the days before antibiotics or political correctness, it was called the Old Man's Friend.

Mary had not seen him, yet. As Davis passed by the open doorways, a patient's name caught his eye. "Charlie Valentine" it said on a neatly printed sign. The name was a blast from the past. In his early years of ministry, he had known a Charlie Valentine. That was when he lived in Hatteras. How many Charlie Valentines could there be?

He stopped at the doorway and looked in. The resident was curled up in his bed. If his mind was gone, his wavy white hair was not. It was one of the outstanding features of Charlie Valentine. The other was a smile that grinned ear to ear.

"Charlie?" said Davis as he moved toward the bed. The man's eyes popped open. "Charlie, it's Davis McGowan, we met years ago in Hatteras. It was on a Habitat for Humanity build."

The smile was still there. Davis wanted to believe that recognition was there, too, but it could have been muscles twitching in familiar patterns.

Charlie was a retired minister when Davis had met him nearly two decades earlier. In the ministry, *retirement* is a relative term. He was still actively preaching in a rural church that could not afford a full-time pastor. In reality, they got the best deal ever. Valentine was the best. He would never have thought so, but a young Davis McGowan aspired to be just like him. What adjectives could he muster? Compassionate, friendly, hard-working, conversational, and tough-minded when it came to the things that mattered. He had learned a lot from Charlie Valentine on that day so long ago, and more during his Hatteras years.

In his mind, Davis went back to that cool, clear morning in the spring. He was helping to nail up a stud wall. It was pleasant work for McGowan who felt more comfortable in a carpenter's apron than a pulpit gown. He had grown up in a family where a man's usefulness was measured in his ability to make things work and fix things that were broken.

Charlie had watched him drive a nail through a two-by-four. It was a simple task that Davis had accomplished by the time he was seven. His own father had given him a hammer and a box of nails while working on a project around the house. Even if it had taken him more than three whacks to drive the nail, he always managed to hit it square. As an adult, Valentine put him through the same test.

"You're going to do fine in the ministry," Charlie had observed. "You know, I've been all around the Ohio Valley during my career and I found that you can get more respect from lay people by driving a nail or sawing a straight line than you can by preaching a sermon."

Charlie's words proved true. Davis was always amazed at the low regard people had for ministers. Oh, they praised their faithfulness and piety, but had very low expectations about anything else that really mattered. It was a strange phenomenon. For the most part, churches had no great budgetary resources, so it fell on the pastor to be a jack-of-all-trades. Davis remembered one day in Hatteras when he had stopped at the bank to arrange for the church's construction loan and then stopped at the hardware store to buy a replacement toilet seat for the stall in the men's room. That pretty much said it all.

Over the years, he had fixed the plumbing, the roofs, the office machines and the phones. On every Habitat day, however, he'd have to prove himself all over again. "Well, Reverend, we could really use some help picking up these scraps of boards and putting them in a pile." There were times when he'd want to strangle someone, but that would not have been a Charlie Valentine sort of thing to do. He'd have quietly picked up his handsaw and cut a straight line. Leadership by example is an old idea that ought to make a comeback.

The grin had not left Charlie's face, so it probably meant much less than it once did. Still, it was something, and Davis felt like a family member holding out against the inevitable. He sat in the chair next to the bed, pulled out a notepad that he always carried and wrote a poem. The words came swiftly and easily:

He looked at his voice,
For it was there that he hoped to recognize him.
Dim eyes betray awareness,
  But the voice was still real.
Names no longer matter,

Gone with all faces.

He looked at his voice.

Vaguely familiar, comforting, without face or name.

He looked at his voice,
But not as one tracing the wispy breath of a cold morning,
Those were images of sight,
They belonged to the eyes.

When memory and vision fade,
one only sees with the ears and remembers with the heart.

He looked at his voice.

What was it? It was familiar, it was safe.

"Don't worry, I'm here!"

"Charlie, I'll visit you again," he said. He meant it, whether or not it would happen. "Charlie, thank you. I owe you more than I could ever repay." He offered a familiar prayer, one that Charlie would have known from the old Book of Common Worship. "Until the busy world is hushed, and the fever of life is over, and our work is done." There was not much else to say. He laid the poem on the nightstand and went back out into the hall.

Mary was still there. When she saw Davis, she called out to him: "I wondered when you would get here today."

False Witness

1

A blast from an approaching train cut through the air of the summer night. Davis could feel its rumbling through the boat's hull as the freight locomotive approached the trestle where the tracks crossed the river. The thunder of the engine's passing was soon replaced by a pattern of clattering as steel wheels bounced along the seams in the rails. He lifted his glass in a toast to the train and to the welcome sound. He laughed to himself and at the simple fact that, in spite of the noise, this was the most peaceful spot on earth that he had ever known.

He swirled the ice in his glass of Famous Grouse, a scotch blend that reminded him of his days in Britain. The day was certainly ending better than it began. He and Beth had planned to get started for vacation early and make the three and a half hour drive to the lake in time to have an afternoon of sailing, but someone had different ideas. More than just *someone*, he thought; death and a coroner's inquest had invited this delay.

"It's just one of the many things that they never teach in seminary," he said out loud to no one.

"What's that?" came an unexpected reply. It was Beth, back from the restroom after a quick shower. Davis was surprised. He hadn't seen her walking along the dock, and her sudden appearance jolted him back to reality.

"Where did you come from?" he responded as his wife stepped into the cockpit of the sailboat.

"I waved as I came along the dock," she said, "but you were obviously in outer space."

"Sorry," he said, "you know me. It takes the first week of vacation to realize that it's started. I must have been in outer space to not notice such a sexy woman! Now that you have my attention, I have to ask, did you ever have an insatiable desire to run away to sea?"

"With you? Always," was her quick reply.

"I want this to just be our time," he said. "Of course, I'm going to have to shake off some of the excess baggage from today!"

"Sounds great!" she said as she leaned over to kiss him. "I am looking forward to having your undivided attention!" The kiss lasted longer than either of them had expected, and they both sensed that the magic of this place was beginning to weave its spell. "Where can a woman get a drink around here, Sailor?" she asked when they came up for air.

"Oops, almost forgot rule number one: When in doubt, ply her with strong drink!" He winked as he rose to his feet and disappeared into the cabin.

"Honey, this one was 'plied' a long time ago!" she said, as he ducked under the hatch cover.

Down below he poured out vodka in a waiting glass, fished into the cooler for a handful of ice, and topped off the drink with tonic. Davis handed the glass through the companionway before he stepped back up into the cockpit. For a while they said nothing as they sat opposite each other and sipped their drinks.

"You know, if they moved the boat storage building, we'd be able to see the sunset right now," he said, breaking the silence. He gestured toward the huge blue structure that rose at the end of the dock.

"Maybe we should ask them to do that for us," she mused.

"Nah, on second thought, then everyone would want to be docked here and the marina fees would go up. Let's keep the storage building, the damn train, and the factory on the other side of the river. Otherwise, everyone will find their way to paradise. This way, it stays disguised and ours!"

"I'll drink to that," Beth retorted with a raising of her glass. They both laughed until silence washed over them.

"You weren't in outer space just now, were you?" she broke the quiet. "You were back in Dayton."

"Yes, I guess it really shook me, today. That's what I was thinking about when I said 'that's one of the things I didn't learn in seminary.'"

"That's what I figured," said Beth.

"I'm used to not getting away on vacation on schedule," began Davis. "I mean, how many times have we crossed our fingers, hoping that none of the people in the hospital will die before we get away? So when Frank died two days ago, I just took it in stride that the funeral service would delay our departure."

"And it's better than getting called back from here, and that's what would have happened if he'd held on longer," added Beth. "You'd have gone back to do the service."

"You're right. For Frank and Alice, I'd give up some vacation rather than having some stranger doing the funeral. I guess I'm just a softie that way."

"And that's why I love you." Silence took over again.

Davis finally broke the stillness. "I just wasn't ready to be served a summons by the sheriff. The family had just left the room, and 'Mr. Sensitivity' walks in to take me to testify before the coroner's jury. He had that subpoena for three days and sat on it. Then he waltzes in and says that I'm to be at the courthouse in thirty minutes. What a jerk! The family's ready for the trip to the cemetery and he wants to whisk off the minister."

"What did you say?"

"I said that I'd be there as soon as I could, and that since I still had thirty minutes, I'd be able to finish my responsibilities before he could legally arrest me for contempt of court."

"You didn't?"

"I sure did! With vacation so close, I guess I was feeling feisty. Oh well, he backed off. On the other hand, he put his patrol car in the procession and drove me to the courthouse after the internment. That's where I was when I called you to say don't worry about leaving too soon."

"And they wanted to know about Angie's death?" Beth asked.

"Yes, they wanted to know everything about her, her illnesses, and about Barker's behavior the night she died."

"What did you say?"

"Mostly I told them what happened that night, but they kept pressing for other things like 'Were they a happy couple?' and 'Did Barker ever talk about euthanasia?' I just told them what I knew and tried to stay away from opinions. I told them how Barker called at about 2:30 a.m. and said that he thought Angie was dead and could I come over. They picked up on that, 'Why did he say that he *thought* she was dead?' I said that I've been in the ministry for over twenty years and I've never had any death call in which a widower didn't say exactly that. I think they aren't ready to say that their wife *is* dead. They seemed disappointed in that answer, and asked me to tell them everything. So I went through the whole thing again. Going up to the room and seeing Angie there, I remember asking Barker if he touched anything, and he said that he hadn't. Then we walked over to the bed, and he said that he never expected this so soon, and he cried. Everyone thought that the cancer treatments would go well and that the prognosis was good even with her diabetes. We said a prayer, and then he started to say again that if he had known she was so close he would have been with her, but he was downstairs watching TV or something. I asked if Matthew knew and he said that he wanted me to help him tell their son, so we went down the hall to wake him up. I think it had to be scary, even for a sixteen-year-old, and he knew something was very wrong when he saw me there.

"The three of us went back to the master bedroom. Matt couldn't stay there long, so we went downstairs, and I called the sheriff's office and then Dr. Carew. They wanted to know Carew's reaction to Angie's death. I said that at 3:30 a.m. all reactions sound alike, but that I thought she was surprised that Angie had died so quickly. On the other hand, she was a diabetic and some tests would tell. She talked to the deputy sheriff a while. After that they asked some polite questions and finally the coroner came. I'd never had that experience. Usually we'd just call the funeral home. Anyway, they removed the body and said that it was okay to go up to the room.

"That was about 6:30, and the Petersons came over from next door and pitched in to help with Matt and Barker. I went upstairs and stripped the bed and took the sheets and washed them. They were soiled. The guy from the prosecutor's office jumped on that like I was destroying evidence or something, but I said that we had the permission of the sheriff's department. They asked if that was normal behavior and, like I said, I was pretty feisty, so I said, sure most people soil the sheets when they die! They weren't real happy with that and said I was a hostile witness. So I gave them a straight answer; I didn't think anyone should have soiled sheets to remind them that their life partner had just died. That's when they asked me if I liked Barker Fornesby. I thought that was a strange question, but I said, 'Yes, as well as I know him.'"

"I can guess their next question," interrupted Beth who had been listening intently. "How well did you know him, Pastor McGowan?"

"You were eavesdropping then," responded Davis. "That's exactly what they asked, and I hate it when they call me 'pastor'. Hey, if I wanted to be called that, I'd be a Lutheran," he said with a wink.

"What did you tell them?"

"I said that from what I had observed, Barker Fornesby was a devoted family man, a competent executive, and not so full of ego that he couldn't laugh at himself. Yes, I liked him, and I trusted him. It's a feeling based on observation from afar. We weren't close socially.

"They followed that by asking: 'Why did he call you first, then?' That was a tough one. I had never really considered that question. Why do some people call their ministers first, even before family? There must be fifty reasons, and I couldn't tell them why Barker would have called me. There are a lot of possibilities. Maybe he feels that he knows the way that I think; he's listened to me long enough. Maybe he trusts me as a person, or maybe he's one of those who thinks ministers walk closer to God than mere mortals... but, I don't think that's it. My guess is that we'd held hands in a circle at Angie's bedside over the years, and if I didn't share his social status, I did understand his fear. Anyway, that's what I said."

"What did they say to that?" asked Beth.

"Actually, they started asking about his real 'social status'. That threw me, because I didn't have a clue about what they were driving at. The guy is a V.P. in a software technologies firm. He's only thirty-nine years old, and his annual bonus exceeds my yearly salary. But then, they started to ask about the group that showed up at Angie's funeral. I think I told you about that, didn't I?"

Beth nodded.

"Apparently some of the stuffed shirts from the corporation were taken back by what they considered 'inappropriate dress' at the funeral. I guess it surprised some that Barker had all sorts of friends, but it didn't surprise me. He never struck me as being class-conscious, and I guess that's why I like him. Oh well, that was my day. Should I write it up in a report: 'What I Did on my Summer Vacation'?"

"Hmm," replied Beth, "only if I get included in the juicy parts!"

"That's right! No more talk of work or Dayton. After all, this is paradise, right? Let's make the boat rock!"

Just then the whistle of another freight train screeched out its warning. Davis and Beth looked at each other and laughed out loud.

"Welcome to paradise, Sailor," she said. And they kissed deeply before going down into the cabin.

2

Barker Fornesby was living in hell. Two days ago he had buried his wife of eighteen years, and now he could not make himself go upstairs to the master bedroom. He hoped that his son Matthew was asleep but he doubted it. He had the urge to go talk to his son, but there was a different grief for each of them. He had lost his wife, Matt lost his mother, and except for the fact that they were one and the same Angela Fornesby, they were different losses.

He looked at the clock and saw that it was nearly 2:00 a.m. It was about this time that he had discovered Angie's body. He recalled that he had been chatting to a computer friend over the Internet. They had been talking about impressions of Disneyworld, and it had been the first time that Barker had laughed since Angie got home from the hospital. His computer friend went by the alias, "Nirvana". His was "Slipped Disk" because, at thirty-nine, he was one of the older users on this board. "Nirvana's" real name was Deb and she was a single parent who worked as an intensive care nurse at an area hospital. Knowing her had been very helpful when his wife was first diagnosed with ovarian cancer. They had met in person several times for lunch, and Deb was able to explain many of the things that the physicians had skipped over with their clinical definitions. By now, Deb knew his moods, and had sensed the need to keep things light on the night that he made the awful discovery. She also knew, but didn't tell him, that the chemotherapy would be particularly tricky since Angie had been a diabetic for many years. But Barker and Angie were so pleased that she was out of the hospital. They believed that she'd do better at home than in the hospital and, if her condition introduced some risk, they had agreed that it was a risk worth taking.

When Angie's death appeared in the paper, it was Deb who notified Barker's other friends in the computer chat room. They had come to the funeral as a group, and Barker was deeply touched. These were people from every walk of life who wanted and expected nothing from him other than friendship, and that was something that he was willing to give.

At 2:00 a.m. the house was empty, devoid of its soul. He would have liked to scream, but the Jack Daniels was close by, and there was some comfort in that. Out of habit more than anything else, he switched on his PC. He watched blankly as the icons rolled across the bottom of the screen. Finally, a pop-up revealed his instant messenger's list of online friends. Barker breathed deeply when he saw that "Nirvana" was on-line.

Before he could enter any keystrokes, his screen scrolled into "chat mode". A steady hand on a keyboard half way across town entered a message:

> *Hi, Barker. I thought you'd be awake now... how are you?*

Barker's fingers stuttered over the keyboard:

> *Better now, Deb. Can we talk?*

The electronic screen beamed Deb's one word response, "Sure," she typed. The invitation gave Barker a chance to type in the question that had been plaguing his mind:

> *I've got a needle here that I need to dispose. Can you take it with you to the hospital? It would be a big favor!*

3

Matt Fornesby was lying awake in the darkness of his room. He could still see, in his mind's eye, every detail that surrounded him, and most of them reminded him of his mother. He could see the fossils that they had collected on their secret forays to the fossil fields when his father was away on business trips. And there were other things as well. He thought that tomorrow he would take down the picture of his family on vacation at Hilton Head. Like many families, they didn't have too many pictures of everyone but, on that particular afternoon, they ran into a family of Japanese tourists. After a series of universally friendly gestures, they exchanged cameras and took group photos. In the picture, Matt stood in the middle with an arm around his mother and father while each of his parents had an arm over his shoulders. They were all smiling. He was fourteen at the time, and his mother had not yet been diagnosed with cancer.

The picture reminded him of happier times, and somehow he felt that he'd let his parents down. Lately, there were too many months without smiles, and he felt the burden of being the cause. There was the episode with the beer keg at a swim party when a friend's parents were out of town. Then he had been merciless about getting his driver's license, and a car. That's when his mother started to get sick. She offered him the mini-van, because she didn't feel up to driving. He remembered throwing the keys against the wall and saying that he wasn't going to drive an "old codger's bus". Why had he said that? His mother was very pretty, and he loved her.

After the funeral, some friends came over to the house, and he had cried when he saw the discolored spot on the drywall where the keys had ricocheted. He wished he hadn't thrown those keys or seen the sad hurt in his mother's eyes.

When his mother was in the hospital, and his Dad stayed with her all night, he had been at home alone. One of those nights, in a flood of tears, he made a deal with God to be a new person. The next day he went to a home center and found out about spackling compound and fixed the dent in the wall. The repair did not match the painted surface, but he considered it a good start on his new resolve. The next night he was alone again, and he decided that he would begin to love something he hated, his mother's insulin syringes.

Matt couldn't remember a time when his mother did not give herself insulin. Her diabetes was treated so matter-of-factly that it was as normal to ask about glucose levels at the dinner table as to say "pass the salt". Yet, there was something ominous about it for Matt. It was as if everything he ever did was conditioned by an overhanging threat that almost seemed normal. He hated that. He remembered taking classes to give insulin. He was thirteen at the time, and the ability to give insulin injections was a sort of rite of passage in his house. Though he had seen it done hundreds of times, it was not a skill that he wanted to master. But master it, he did. He learned the use of a glucose meter to calculate the dosage and how to fill the syringe. His graduation was when he actually gave a dose to his mother. He was so afraid that he would hurt her, but she smiled and said he had done fine. His father had been very clinical. "This is something we all must be able to do in an emergency, and we do it because we love your mother."

Now he was sixteen, nearly seventeen, and that night alone in his room he vowed to God that he would be a loving son. If his mother came home from the hospital, he would do anything to make her well again, even if it meant facing his enmity toward the needle. In the middle of the night he went to find the instructions to the glucose meter, and fell asleep reading them. The next day, his father found them on the kitchen table when he came home from the hospital, and was proud of his son's intent.

The night his mother died, he had given her the insulin she needed. She had spent the day nauseated from the chemo and her blood sugar was rising. Dr. Carew was also concerned about dehydration, and a visiting nurse came to set up an IV drip. The nurse found Angie's glucose reading to be elevated to around 560. His dad went to talk with the nurse as she was leaving, and his mother suggested that he test his skill by using the glucose meter and testing his reading against the nurse's. Matt was pleased when his own calculations matched. "560 it is," he stated proudly.

"That's great, honey," his mother said.

"Should I fill the syringe, or did the nurse already give you the injection?" he asked.

"No she didn't, Matt. Would you do it for me? Just mark the chart so that your father knows." Matt was trembling, but he checked and double checked the dose, and carefully recorded it on the log that his father was keeping. His mother appreciated her son's kindness. He hoped that his awkwardness with the needle did not hurt her.

"Never worry about me," she said. "I am just so proud of my son and my husband. They are two very kind and caring men." Matt warmed from within at her words and kissed her goodnight. It was the last time he saw her alive, and at 3:00 a.m. he would be awakened to a nightmare by his father and Dr. McGowan.

Now, in the darkness, he kept going over and over the turn of events. He could not help but think that he had done something wrong. His mother was dead, and surely there must be someone to blame.

4

In ancient times, great glaciers scraped flat the terrain of the western portion of Ohio leaving the flat fertile plains that human civilization would transform into the farm belt. The remnants of this period were evident to Dr. Davis McGowan who lived near the glacier's terminal moraine that marked a dividing line between the rolling hills of southern Ohio and the open lowlands north of Dayton. He was grateful to the forces of time and ice, for they also carved out the Great Lakes, the most underrated sailing waters in the world, at least as far as he was concerned. He and Beth had sailed for more than fifteen years and, having learned the craft at a sailing school on the Chesapeake Bay, had steered clear of Lake Erie because of its reputation for storminess. After years of small lake sailing, frustration over the lack of wind and water overcame their fears of gale force winds. An afternoon of sailing on a charter dissolved all apprehensions, and within a week they had found an old cruiser/racer that would put them out on the water without bankrupting their future.

They found a marina on the St. Clair River that suited their tastes. They shunned the Sandusky Bay which was plagued with the chop from a legion of resident powerboats, and took refuge in a small coastal town to the east. The scenery was not as picturesque, with the west bank of the river for the marinas and shops, and the eastern side for the remnants of a more industrial age when Great Lakes shipping reached its zenith.

They were less than a mile up the river, just past the municipal boat basin in a working marina called North Haven. It was owned by a family and had a friendly atmosphere that extended to the whole work force. Upstream was the roadway and train overpass that marked the extent of sailboat navigation, though several powerboat marinas were located beyond.

Some of the people knew Davis' profession, but most kept it to themselves, so that the Reverend Doctor could share the luxury of being a "normal" person when in port. Aside from an occasional joke about fixing the weather, no one paid much attention to the middle-aged couple who were so obviously in love with sailing and with each other. Most did not guess that they were in their late forties with grown children of their own. They seemed more like newlyweds with a playfulness that made others envious. To Davis and Beth, North Haven was a retreat from the expectations and judgments of others. They lived their daily lives in a fishbowl, but here they felt that they had their true life.

Though Davis' mind went back to the coroner's inquest from time to time, Beth could see his youthfulness returning already, and laughter was coming easier to them both.

"I'm scared for Barker," said Davis, at last.

"Why's that? Because of the medical examiner's report? Couldn't it still be an accident?" asked Beth.

"Of course it was an accident," replied Davis. "Angie and he were in such good spirits at the hospital. She was developing imaging techniques to get her through the chemo. I even suggested that if she really felt rotten she should try thinking of a fierce battle between the chemo and the cancer, and the worse she felt the greater a licking the cancer cells were getting. She even laughed at that one and said that she was going to call the tumor 'George Armstrong Custer'! They were very good together and not about to give up hope."

"Well, then, there shouldn't be anything to worry about, right?" queried Beth.

"I guess not. But when the cause of death was listed as cardiac arrest brought on by hypoglycemia, well something didn't look right. I mean somebody had to give her a lot more insulin than she needed."

"And that points to Barker."

"Or to suicide," responded Davis.

"I never thought of that," puzzled Beth. "But wouldn't she have left a note? I mean, I'd leave one just to say goodbye to my family so that they wouldn't have to have so many questions."

"That would be my guess, too. They were too close a family for her to just check out without at least a love note to Barker. That's why I'm worried. It was either a big accident or murder. My hunch is accident, but what a thing for Barker and Matt to have to face."

"Okay, Davis McGowan, you are a mother hen, and you can call the office every three days, but no more often! Barker is totally capable, and he will be fine, but you will flip a gasket if you don't start taking care of yourself a little."

"Yes, Doctor, and what medicine do you prescribe?"

"Hmm, that's easy! Sun, sailing, and me!" she said kissing him on the nose. "But not necessarily in that order."

"Sounds like a perfect diagnosis, and a wonderful cure!"

5

Bill Slater could not get the coroner's report of Angela Fornesby's death out of his mind. "I'll bet the bastard gets away with it," he thought. He'd only met Barker Fornesby a few times, but didn't like him. To him, Barker had led the charmed life of the advantaged. This was in contrast to his own trip through law school, which was haltingly slow. It had taken him years to pay off his student loans on his salary as an attorney in the prosecutor's office. The whole system favored those with the advantages of money and power. Had this been anyone else, the press would have been having a field day with the coroner's finding that

Angela Fornesby's death was not from natural causes. As it was, not a word had appeared, though it had been ten days since her death and a week since the autopsy report showed that the cause of death was an overdose of insulin.

The other thing that bothered Slater was the way in which everyone seemed to want to find reasonable explanations to dismiss the report as being trivial. He had found himself in a ridiculous argument with the coroner because Dr. Jacobs was wavering about sending his findings to a grand jury.

"What's the difference between an insulin syringe and a gun?" he asked facetiously. "If she were shot you'd be here trying to explain how she fell on the bullet. Forget that this is one of your society cronies. A woman is dead, and someone put the poison in her. Let the grand jury decide if there's been a crime."

In the end, his logic prevailed. He felt a little smug as Marty Jacobs ordered that the autopsy report be sent up to the grand jury to see if there was any evidence of a crime.

"Oh," said Marty as they ended their debate, "you might find out if the investigating officer found an insulin log kept by the family. I have the physician's orders and the notes from the visiting nurse, but all the answers might be in that one missing link." Slater smiled with satisfaction. Now it was in his hands.

6

In spite of what Bill Slater thought, Marty Jacobs, the county coroner, was a competent forensic specialist. In any case, even someone with less experience would have easily determined the cause of Angela Fornesby's death. A routine blood test determined high insulin levels, and the rest was simple deduction resulting from a chain reaction of events. Too much insulin leads to insulin shock, an induced hypoglycemia that can trigger cardiac arrhythmia and death. He also knew that there could be explanations other than murder or manslaughter that would explain this progression. The overdose could have been accidental or fluctuations in her glucose levels could have been affected by the chemotherapy or she may have started showing signs of becoming insulin resistant with larger and larger doses being necessary to control sugar levels. It would be easy to over calculate dosages with so many variables.

That scenario was the most likely, and was the compelling reason why he was in no hurry to release his findings. He owed it to his friend, Barker Fornesby, not to be too quick in sounding any alarms. Even before the report was typed, he had called Barker on the phone warning him that there were some unanswered questions which would have to be dealt with. It was a difficult phone call coming so quickly on the heels of Angie's death, even before final arrangements for the memorial service could be announced.

"Barker, I hate to tell you this, but it appears that insulin shock triggered Angie's heart failure. I'm going to need some documentation from you before I can release a statement. Without it, the report will raise as many questions as it answers. Did you keep a log of her glucose levels and insulin?"

"Of course," was Barker's quick reply, "it's around here somewhere. Things are a little out of sorts."

"I understand, Barker. Look, I can hold up my report for a while, but I'll need to talk to some folks about what happened, and I need that log. I'd like to keep this low-keyed with no formal coroner's jury or anything, okay?"

The voice at the other end of the line hesitated, "I understand, Marty. You have to do what you have to do, and I'll do the same."

"Look, I'm really sorry about this, but if you appear to take the initiative, fewer eyebrows will be raised. This can be handled quickly and quietly, I'm sure."

"Thanks, Marty, I'll see what I can do. You're a friend."

"You'd do the same for me. How's Matt handling all this?" They continued to talk for a while, and Marty's opinion of Barker was only strengthened by the tenor of their conversation. He could not conceive of any untoward action by his friend of many years. The two had served on community boards, and United Way fund drive committees together, and their continuing interest in the well-being of the community had given Marty Jacobs a strong idea of what his friend was capable of doing by will or by devotion.

But now the issue was being pushed by Bill Slater. Marty puzzled as to why Barker had not been forthcoming with the insulin log. He had stretched his neck out a long way with the first phone call, and would have to follow the book from here on out. Slater was right about one thing,

Marty was stalling and looking for any way to not make an issue out of a question that clearly needed an answer.

7

Deputy Jake Dudek was on duty the night that Angela Fornesby died, and so it was his report that was on the desk of Sheriff Jerry Gardner. The sheriff had read the report, but put it aside until Bill Slater, from the prosecutor's office, phoned. The brief conversation hit like a ton of bricks. Nothing in the deputy's report had indicated anything abnormal or suspicious, but now the words "grand jury" and "first degree murder" made him leap to attention. A crucial piece of evidence was missing, and Deputy Dudek's report had made no mention of a log kept by the family. Slater's tone was conciliatory, and Sheriff Gardner soon felt himself to be an ally in a campaign to unmask a conspiracy of murder. The sheriff was equally sure that his deputy, Jake Dudek, would be able to determine why Barker Fornesby was not willing to supply the document.

The deputy would be coming on duty soon, and his first order of the day would be to report directly to the sheriff for a special assignment. The trail of evidence was cold now, especially in an investigation that was from the outset so routine. If Dudek were to uncover anything at this late date, it would take the finesse of a skilled observer. Dudek fit the bill. He had served in the Marines as a young man and had found that law enforcement fit his bearing and temperament. He was a large, intimidating man who preferred action to paperwork. Today, his instructions would be quite different from that early morning hour when he was met at the door by the Fornesby's minister and led to the master bedroom where Angela lay dead. If his powers of observation had been blunted that day, it was because of the mood that hung over the house when he entered. The thought now hit him that that may have been a veneer that disguised the real purposes at work. That at least was the concern of the prosecutor's office, and Jake Dudek would find that a more comfortable role than that of the consoling duty officer. In his own defense, everything that night told him to be quick and courteous and cut through the "red tape". The minister's presence, the silently mournful teenager, and the call to the physician who was surprised by the suddenness of the death, but moved to genuine sympathy for the burden of the family, all worked together to set a tone that was difficult to penetrate. Now Jake Dudek was to go back and to direct his gaze, not on a stricken widower, but on a clever man capable of concealing a murder and motive.

8

Davis McGowan sat up in his berth and leaned his back against the bulkhead that divided the forward cabin of his boat from the adjacent compartment. Next to him Beth was sleeping peacefully. In the darkness, he could hear her regular breathing. It was music added to the chorus of the water lapping against the hull.

Angie Fornesby's death had taken its toll on him. It was a subtle kind of awareness that haunted him when he sat up alone at night. He thought of what his own life would be if it had been his wife who died, and not Barker's. It was not a thought that he wanted to entertain. Most people thought that the crises of a minister's life revolved around issues of faith, but most people were wrong. The single strongest enemy in Davis' life was loneliness.

The questions from the coroner's jury paraded in his mind: "Why did he call you first?" and "How well do you know him?"

The answers were so simple as they played out in Davis' consciousness: "He called me because I am his minister." and "I know him well enough to know that what most people think of Barker Fornesby is not true."

To most people Barker seemed calculating, organized, decisive, and not given to emotional arguments. Davis had seen another side to the man. He had seen a man holding Angie's hand while she slept in a hospital bed. He had seen a man with tears in his eyes after a prayer, and he had seen his stricken look the night Angie died. They were only momentary glimpses of a man who always seemed to be able to take charge and make things happen.

"I wonder if people feel the same way about me?" pondered Davis. As a minister he was invited into people's lives at intensely personal and emotional times. He was the conduit through which they vented anger and fear and grief. When coping became possible, they turned back to their lives which did not include him. Over the years so many people had commented on how close they felt to him and how grateful they were for his kindness. Yet, he knew that they knew absolutely nothing about him as a human being. He was their minister, but they seldom asked him what he felt or liked or even if he had brothers or sisters.

Church fights were another thing. Anger over church policy was always directed toward him, and he felt the burden of bringing people to understanding when he could. He hated congregational meetings when he would be excused while several hundred people considered whether or not his salary should be increased. Once, he had been publicly accused of violating the church constitution by a member who had been set-up to lead the attack with a half-truth. Later investigation proved that the charge was false, but no public apology was ever offered. He was a functionary, and always on the verge of losing his sense of self.

Beth was his anchor, the one person who really knew him. People often marveled at the closeness of their marriage, but it was no mystery. She seemed to be the only one who accepted that he was an ordinary person. Being married to him was not an easy life. At times the expectations flowed over both of them until she too wanted to have an identity of her own and not be known as "Mrs. McGowan, the minister's wife." Davis could not blame her for that, but it only heightened his own isolation. He knew other pastors of large churches. Like him, they were shunned by their peers who felt less successful. Many of them had become caricatures of themselves, or closet alcoholics. Some had even become involved in sexual misconduct. It seemed like the public delighted in exposing such failure, but these were just lonely people who had tried to give more than they could, and lost themselves.

In the darkness, Davis felt tears rolling down his cheeks. As carefully as possible, he slipped out of the double berth and went aft to the main cabin. Among the navigational charts, he found a pencil and paper and began to write:

How many kinds of sunshine are there?
Is it all harsh glow,
    or filtered shadow?
And if I should stand in one light,
    and you in another,
   does the one that bathes you become less
     revealing?
Suppose the same light would cover us both,
    even for a minute.
In that speck of time,
    we would see alike
      with all being clear,
        with all being bright.
Come close, or let me take your hand,
    for walking together in this time
     seems like life to me,
    and sharing the light,

earth's fairest dream.

He copied the poem carefully, then set it on the counter where Beth would find it in the morning. He returned to the forward cabin and climbed into the berth. Beth stirred.

"Can't you sleep?" she said.

"I was up for a bit. I think I'll sleep now," he answered. He rolled next to her and wrapped his arm around her. She snuggled back against him and drifted off to sleep. Silent tears welled up beneath Davis' closed eyelids, and then sleep took him as well.

9

"Have you gotten any word from Barker Fornesby?" came the voice of Bill Slater over the phone.

"No, nothing," answered Marty Jacobs, the coroner.

"Not even the insulin log?" continued Slater.

"No, but I'm sure he's just forgotten about it," apologized Jacobs.

"You've got to stop making excuses for him, Marty. I think the guy's hiding something."

"But why? What possible motive can he have?"

"How about money or sex... maybe he has a girlfriend waiting in the wings? You really have to quit being so naive, Marty."

"I think you've been watching too many detective movies, Bill. Just leave the guy alone. There's nothing there to prosecute."

"I guess that's my decision, isn't it?" replied Slater, as he hung up the phone without waiting for an answer. He wondered about the power that this man, Barker Fornesby, wielded so easily to create such depth of loyalty.

10

Barker was clearly shaken when he had gotten off the phone with Marty Jacobs. The coroner had promised himself that he would cease any interference in the investigation of Angela Fornesby's death, but the call from Bill Slater had set him off.

In this second call, he warned Barker to find the insulin log and to beware of a zealot from the prosecutor's office who would like to throw his hat into the political ring by uncovering a first class scandal. Fornesby remembered the name from some earlier meeting, but could not picture this person who was so clearly aligning himself to be his nemesis. Nervously, he got off the phone with Marty Jacobs, and took several deep breaths to bring back his composure. Contrary to the coroner's excuses on his behalf, he had not forgotten the insulin log. He had not risen to be a corporate vice president by forgetting details or leaving things to chance. He picked up the receiver of his desk phone and entered the four digit extension to one of his departments. A man answered.

"Ted? This is Barker, are you alone? Good! I'm on my way down to your office. I need to talk about a security matter." With that he hung up the phone. Ted

Clarke was a good security chief, but he had also retired from the Sheriff's Office three years earlier when Barker had hired him. He still had some contacts that might be useful.

"Margaret, I'll be down in security for a half hour or so," he said as he walked past his secretary's desk. "You can't find me, unless it's Matt, alright?"

"Sure, Boss," she said as she flashed him a friendly smile. The confidence had returned to his voice. He seemed more like his old self at that moment, she thought.

11

Ted Clarke and Barker were well into a discussion of Bill Slater and his political ambitions when the phone on the desk rang out. The sound brought an abrupt end to a serious conversation between Fornesby and the ex-cop.

"It's Margaret, for you," said Clarke handing the handset to Barker.

"Hello, Margaret," Barker said taking the phone, "Is it Matt?" Clarke could only hear half of the conversation.

"Oh, okay..."

"No, I think you did the right thing, just transfer the call to me down here." Barker shifted a little and cleared his throat. The next transaction showed a change in his voice and manner as he was clearly talking to someone else.

"No problem, Deputy. I can be there in fifteen minutes. Okay, I'll see you then. Bye for now." He hung up the phone.

"Who was that?" asked Ted Clarke.

"The Deputy that came to the house the night Angie died. His name is Dudek."

"Jake Dudek," added Clarke. "He's a good soldier. What did he want?"

"Wants to meet me at the house in fifteen minutes."

"Oh, returning to the scene," commented Clarke. "Smells like Bill Slater to me! But you'll never make it in fifteen minutes."

"I know," answered Fornesby. "I want him to be there when I get there."

"Good thinking, Boss." Barker was nearly out the door by now and headed back toward his office to get his suit coat and tell Margaret to clear his schedule.

12

The patrol car was waiting in the drive when Barker pulled in at about 3 p.m. Deputy Dudek opened the car door and extricated his hulking body from the automobile as Fornesby's car made the turn. The garage door began to swing open by remote control.

"Sorry to be late," apologized Barker.

"No problem, I've only just arrived myself," said the officer.

"Angie would go crazy if I brought company in through the garage," said Barker, "but I'm afraid that I don't even carry a house key these days. Hope you don't mind?"

Already Jake was finding it difficult to maintain a suspicious attitude toward Barker. "Of course, I don't mind," he answered. They went in through a neat garage. One corner housed a work bench with a few tools left out. Bicycles lined one of the three car stalls, and gardening tools hung neatly from the wall. From the garage they entered the house through a mud room that opened into the kitchen.

"Can I get you a soft drink or anything, Officer?" asked Barker.

"I'm just a deputy, sir, but no thank you," came the well-trained reply. "Mostly I have come to collect an insulin log and to look around one more time. It's just routine. I need to make a sketch of the room arrangement and that sort of thing. I really don't like to intrude."

"No need to explain," offered Barker. "I'd forgotten about that insulin log. I guess it's upstairs in the bathroom where it was when you were here last. Come with me."

The two walked through the neatly kept house and climbed the stairs to the master bedroom suite. Barker kept close to the deputy. Once inside the room, he stopped. The bed was still unmade, stripped of the bedclothes.

"I must admit that I haven't been in here much since the other night. It's pretty much the same as when you left it. I need to have the housekeeper straighten it up. The log should be in here." He started for the small door in the corner of the room. At each moment he was in Dudek's sight. "Here it is," he said taking a white sheet of ruled paper from the counter. "I hope it's what you're looking for," he said as he handed it over. "Can I get you anything else?"

"No, you've been very cooperative," replied Dudek. "If you don't mind, I need to make those sketches I told you about. Then I'll be finished. There's no need for you to stay here, if you've something else to do."

Barker took the hint, "No problem, I'll just go down to see what's left in the refrigerator for dinner. The neighbors have been keeping Matt and me well-fed." With that, he left the room.

Jake began to study the room with a keener attention to detail. It was much the same as he remembered. He had not, however, remembered seeing a ruled sheet of white paper in the bathroom and wondered how he could have missed it. Something else was missing too, but at first he could not identify what it was. He had the feeling that a piece of the puzzle was not there, and then it hit him. There were no used syringes. He began a closer inspection of the room, this time looking with a defined purpose. He searched the small bathroom, finding a box of unused sharpies, but no stash of used needles that would have to be disposed of with all the caution of other forms of medical waste.

He returned to the bedroom and began a methodical search of the nightstand, the dresser drawers, and under the furniture. The room was clean. In the corner of the nightstand he saw a blinking light indicating messages on an answering machine. He walked to the door to make sure the hall was clear, and closed the door behind him. Walking to the flashing light, he turned the volume to low and pressed the message retrieval button. Slowly he increased the volume:

"Barker, this is Deb. It's Wednesday at 2 p.m. I'll still be at work at the hospital until 6:00. You can give me a call. It will ring in at the nurses' station. Ask for me. It's 555-8241 and dinner at the Peasant Stock sounds wonderful. Just let me know the time. Are you sure it would be good for us to be seen in public so soon? I could fix dinner at my place. Just let me know! I'll be waiting for your call." The machine logged off with a loud beep and Jake pressed the "save message" button and readjusted the volume. Jake smiled at this unexpected turn of events. He left the bedroom and found Barker in the kitchen checking the contents of plastic storage containers.

"Everything okay?" asked Barker.

"Fine, sir, in fact, I'm just leaving." Barker walked the officer to the door. "Oh," Jake added, "your answering machine in the bedroom was indicating that you had a message. I thought you might miss it, seeing how you've not been up there much."

"Thank you, I'll check," said Fornesby, as he opened the door. "I don't know if I thanked you for your kindness the other night. Things were very confused, but you were very professional and it helped in a difficult time."

Jake paused at the door. "Can I ask one more thing?" he said.

"Sure," answered Barker.

"What procedure did you follow for disposing of your sharpies? I didn't see any used needles in the room." Jake watched for a change in Barker's expression, but his answer seemed very matter of fact.

"We always saved them in a coffee can and took them to the Board of Health every other month or so. I suppose that there aren't any left because the visiting nurse took them when she left the night that Angie died."

Jake hesitated, then took on a self-disgusted look. "I can't believe it," he said. "I've left my notes up in the bedroom." He quickly headed back toward the stairs, calling back to Barker. "I'll just be a minute. It's been one of those days."

"I know what you mean," answered Barker, who was startled by the large man's quickness. He made no attempt to follow.

Jake closed the door behind him, and stood very still. He slowly scanned the room again. He was not looking for his notes. He had feigned forgetfulness in order to search the room again. If Barker was truthful when he said that the visiting nurse had taken all the used needles, it would have meant that the lethal injection was given prior to her leaving on the night in question. In the deputy's opinion that was unlikely. More likely was the possibility that the dose was given after the nurse left, when no one was around to observe an adverse reaction to the medication. If so, there would have been an extra syringe to dispose of. By now it could be anywhere, and finding it in the room seemed very remote. Still, he had to look in this room and broaden the search if it didn't turn up. Perhaps it would take the shape of a melted glob of plastic in the fireplace, or be forever lost in the wilderness of the county landfill, disguised in household garbage. Barker did not seem the type to dispose of medical waste inappropriately.

"Perhaps that will be his downfall," thought Jake. "A conscientious man sits at a red light in the wee hours of the morning when no one else is on the road. Maybe Barker Fornesby's sense of responsibility would not allow him to dispose of a syringe easily, and the needle would not be beyond discovery."

He got down on his hands and knees and circled the bed. At one point he lifted the corner of the mattress. What he saw stopped him cold. There it was. Right in front of him was an unsheathed insulin syringe wedged between the mattress and the box springs. Carefully, he lifted the mattress clear of the corner of the bed. It looked quite harmless lying there, but the fact remained that his search may have uncovered the actual murder weapon, as deadly as a loaded revolver.

Jake studied the hypodermic carefully. The plastic cylinder did not show any visible distortion, and the plunger was fully depressed. Its location seemed puzzling, particularly since Barker had been so specific about his disposal precautions. The removal of the sharpie was in accordance with textbook procedures. He maneuvered the syringe into a small evidence bag and wrapped it so that he could conceal it under his tunic without risk of puncture.

No sooner than he had finished, Barker knocked gingerly on the door. "Everything okay?" came Barker's inquiry.

"Just fine," answered the officer. He would have liked to ask questions, but thought better of that. The questions could wait until the lab had done its own investigative magic. With only the merest exchange of pleasantries, he walked to the front door and left the house. The door closed behind him.

Once outside, he smiled to himself. "Bill Slater will be very interested in this report," he thought. In his pocket was an overlooked syringe, and in his mind was the knowledge of at least four inconsistencies that left him uneasy. An insulin log had materialized in a place where it had not been on the night of Angela's death. Fornesby was pretending to fix supper when he'd already made a date for dinner with a woman named Deb who wasn't sure they should be seen together, and there was only one message on a machine in a room that supposedly had remained untouched for over a week. But the real find was the syringe. If Fornesby was telling the truth and all the used needles went with the nurse, the lethal dose could have been administered by this unaccounted needle sometime after the nurse left the house that night. This fit with the fact that nothing irregular was noted in the nurse's report. Very likely, the packet he carried in his pocket was the instrument of Angela Fornesby's death.

Slater was right about one thing. This man, Barker Fornesby, knew more than he was saying. He had charm, but he also had a secret.

13

"At last I'm getting somewhere," thought Bill Slater as he hung up the telephone. Deputy Jake Dudek had sounded animated about the timely details that he had uncovered. The insulin log was in Barker Fornesby's own hand and seemed unremarkable, but he would send it along with a written report. More hopeful was the syringe found stuffed under the mattress. The lab might discover something about it that would be telling, perhaps a fingerprint or traces of human tissue on the needle. In the meantime, he had the name and number of a woman named Deb who would be meeting Barker this evening. Slater caught some of the excitement of the moment. Yes it was circumstantial, but it was something. He picked up his phone and punched in the numbers that Jake had given him. The phone rang several times before a woman answered.

"Intensive Care, Pod C," came the answer.

"Is Deb there?" asked Slater.

"She's with a patient, right now. Is there anything I can help you with, or can she call you back?"

"No, that's quite alright," said Slater, "I'll call her later. Thanks." He hung up the phone. "The mystery woman exists, then," reflected Slater. "What I need is another angle," he said to himself as he laid out the reports contained in the Fornesby file on the desk in front of him. The medical report from Dr. Carew caught his eye. "It's a long shot, but why not?" He retrieved his phone and entered the doctor's office number. A receptionist answered.

"This is Bill Slater of the Prosecutor's Office. I'm doing a routine overview of the details of Angela Fornesby's death, and was wondering if Dr. Carew was available to talk right now, or give me a call back this afternoon?"

"One moment, and I'll check for you," recited the female voice with practiced precision. The line went silent for a short time until the voice returned. "The doctor can talk with you right now. Let me transfer you."

Before he could acknowledge anything the line began to ring, and a second woman answered. "This is Deborah Carew, how can I help you?"

"Dr. Carew, this is Bill Slater from the Prosecutor's Office. I've just received Angela Fornesby's insulin log, the one kept by the family, and wanted to go over a few details. Do you remember the case?"

"Of course, Mr. Slater. Did you get my report?"

"Yes, Doctor. It was very complete. I am just trying to determine if any of these things can explain the source of the insulin that sent Mrs. Fornesby into shock. According to your report, you gave orders to compensate for the IV therapy by administering insulin with the IV solution. Is that right?"

"Yes it is, Angie... ah, Mrs. Fornesby was nauseated and not able to keep anything down. She was in danger of dehydration, so I ordered IV therapy. Because of her diabetes, we had the solutions prepared with insulin so that the dextrose would not throw off her sugar counts."

"I just wanted to be sure that I understood the report," said Slater. Then he asked the real question that

71

had bothered him. "What would you say Mrs. Fornesby's state of mind was like? Was she depressed?"

"Not at all! Both she and her husband were quite positive, in fact," answered Carew.

"Is there anyone else in the medical community who would know what they were sensing? Say, one of the nurses who attended Mrs. Fornesby in the hospital? Wasn't there a Deb in Intensive Care? I think Barker mentioned her?"

There was a long silence. "No, I don't think that's right," answered Carew, thoughtfully. "Angie wasn't in Intensive Care, unless you're thinking of Deb Walker? Barker seemed to know her from somewhere. Once when I was looking to speak to him during rounds, I found him in a lounge area talking to her very seriously, but she wasn't Angie's nurse."

"Well, thank you, Doctor. You've been very helpful, and I apologize for taking you from your patients."

"Glad to help, Mr. Slater. The Fornesby's are nice people. If you have any other questions, give me a call."

"Sure thing, thanks again," said Slater as he hung up the phone. "Barker Fornesby may be as pleasant a murderer as you'd ever want to know," he thought out loud.

14

Bill Slater had always been a zealot for justice. He was, however, one of those people born out of time sequence. In the late 1960's or early seventies he would have been considered an idealistic youth with ideas of championing the rights of the poor and the oppressed. He could have easily aspired to be an opponent of consumer fraud. To him, Ralph Nader led the ideal life of justice. He could see himself, in his law school years, taking the cases that others would pass over as being unprofitable. Unfortunately for Bill Slater, he attended law school in the eighties and his classmates aspired to a more upscale lifestyle. His wife agreed with the majority and left him early in the fourth year of their marriage.

He found that he could lose himself in his work at the prosecutor's office, and in doing so, never had to face the issue of his personal happiness. Slowly he made his life choices as his identity as a man merged with his identity as an attorney. It was a transformation that he would have denied had he been faced with it point blank. Nevertheless, it was what his life had become. In the lounge at the Peasant Stock that thought struck him, as he waited for Barker Fornesby and Deb Walker to arrive. The room was comfortably full of couples, waiting for tables or just enjoying a cocktail while listening to classical guitar playing in the background. The experience represented a part of his life that was nearly forgotten. His was the pursuit of justice at any cost, and the cost was dearer than he imagined.

He ordered another martini. From the bar in the lounge he could look through French doors and see the restaurant patrons arriving. At about 7:30, Barker and Deb arrived. To Slater they seemed a striking couple which only fueled his suspicions. While they did not hold hands or touch, they seemed very aware of each other. It was only a moment or two before their table was ready, but in that time, Slater could see that they both laughed easily and found comfort in each other's company.

After another drink, Slater could not resist the opportunity to walk through the restaurant. He spied them in a corner booth seated opposite one another. Their discussion was serious, and at one moment, Deb reached out for Barker's hand. He did not pull away, but they continued to talk quietly as though nothing else in the world had any power or existence. Their apparent affection left Slater cold. He left the restaurant with a heightened sense of indignation, but no self-awareness of the real source of his anger.

15

The McGowans were sitting at anchor in Put-in-Bay near South Bass Island. It was here in early September of 1813 that Oliver Hazard Perry received word that the British navy was on the move. Perry weighed anchor to engage the enemy. When the bombardment began, Perry was aboard his flagship, the *Lawrence*. By the end of the Battle of Lake Erie, the *Lawrence* was sunk and Perry had transferred by open boat to the *Niagara*. When the smoke cleared on September 10th, the British fleet had surrendered and Perry had dispatched his immortal message to his superiors, "We have met the enemy and they are ours."

How different the bay seemed as the sun arose over the Perry victory monument.   Davis and Beth were anchored in their small sloop.   It was the last day of their holiday and neither wanted it to end.   At night, Put-in-Bay has a reputation for being rather noisy with live bands and partiers filling the bars and clubs along the bay front.   In the morning, the carousers sleep and the protected waters are returned to the custody of the Great Blue Herons and the gulls.

Davis had awakened early and left Beth asleep in the v-berth.   In the main cabin, he boiled water on the alcohol stove, a device contrived by the devil or, at least, by a sadist.   Whoever first said "A watched pot never boils" must have been cooking with alcohol.   But those have to be watched because of their reputation for flaring up.   He did manage to boil the water without lighting the curtains, and poured out two cups of tea.   Beth was still asleep, so he climbed out on deck to wait while it steeped.

An old barge swung at anchor off his port side on the north side of the bay.   To starboard was a collection of boats that made a representative sample of the Great Lakes fleet.   Ranging in size from about 23 to 37 feet, they all drifted at their own pace to the changes in wind.   With a wind shift the lighter boats respond quickly while the deep-keeled boats come around more slowly.   Boats 50 feet apart one minute can pass within a few feet when the wind changes, and nervous owners worry about tangled anchor lines and sudden thumps in the night.

This morning all was going well.   The water ballet was in harmony with very little to arouse a sleepy yachtsman.

The sky was clear, and the air cool, but not as cool as the dew that Davis sat in on the wet deck. He didn't care. He sat on the forward hatch with his back against the mast and watched the morning dance of the boats and the wind.

"Good morning," called Beth from below. "What's the day like?"

"It's perfect," he answered. "What do you say that we not go back?" he said, moving aft toward the cockpit and then through the companionway and into the cabin.

"Fine with me!" she said. By then he was taking the tea bags out of the cups and adding milk and sugar. He took the hot cups forward to where she was lying in the berth. She sat up and took a cup from him. "I'm sorry it's over," she reflected.

"Me too," he sighed. "But we don't have to be in any hurry to get back. What do you say that we take the long way back by sailing northeast and in sight of Pelee Island? That way we'll have sailed in foreign waters." They both enjoyed the fact that sailing on Erie meant the freedom to travel to another country.

"You know, I read somewhere that our treaty with Canada states that the most powerful armament on the Great Lakes is limited to an eighteen pound cannon," said Davis.

"You're joking?"

"No, it's one of the most effective treaties in history, too. It was negotiated between the United States and the British crown after the War of 1812 and the language was never updated to take into account newer weapons. So the

76

treaty is all wrong with regard to technology, but has a long lasting spirit that hasn't been broken."

There was a long silence as the two of them sipped their tea. Davis reached up and pushed open the overhead hatch. Cool fresh air flooded the cabin and the morning light made them blink for a moment. He retrieved a chart book from the shelf that ran along the perimeter of the v-berth. He opened to the page that showed the western islands and quickly estimated the route they would take to sail close to Pelee Island which lies entirely in Canadian waters. Though not required or strictly legal, they would raise a courtesy flag as they crossed into the Canadian part of the lake. A courtesy flag is the national ensign of the country in whose territory you are traveling. It would not have been necessary to fly the red maple leaf since they were not actually making landfall or clearing customs, but it was always a symbol of pride to Beth and Davis that they had crossed the national boundary by sail.

It was always difficult to face the last day of vacation. Back home, their lives were not their own. What they did and where they went was a matter for public scrutiny. Matters of importance in their own household always had to take second place to the crises in other families. It was worthwhile work, but Davis was aware that his family had paid the real price of his career choice. Being on the boat had become their way of blocking out a world of expectations and a way to rediscover the human beings that were held dormant by time and expectation during the year.

The day itself proved to be picture perfect. The steady fifteen knot breezes and the three foot waves made the sail invigorating and the sloop slid along near hull speed for the next five hours. Neither Davis nor Beth wanted to admit that the destination of this pleasurable sail was a three and a half hour car ride back to reality. It was over all too soon, and they were standing on the dock running over the list of details to secure the boat and pack the car, hoping that at the last minute, something would be remembered that would let them remain a little longer.

At last they were headed west on Route 2 through light traffic. Neither spoke, but they knew that they were feeling the same things, satisfaction at two wonderful weeks, and regret that it was so soon over. Davis turned on the radio. "Might as well have some music before the Cleveland radio stations fade and we're left with country music," said Davis.

"We can probably get back for a few days before the fall, can't we?" asked Beth.

"I sure would like to think so," said Davis. They both doubted it, however.

The drive between St. Clair and Dayton was over flat farmland and through small towns. The only real curiosity for the couple was the various farm vehicles that they would see at different times during the growing season. Sometimes they would have to guess the function of a particular piece of equipment that would explain the strangeness of the design. Some of the equipment, thought Davis, looked like it was straight out of "Star Wars", but they never saw any white-armored storm troopers, just red faced men and women with ball caps and a look of tired determination.

16

The lab report on the mysterious syringe did not give Bill Slater much to go on. It had been a long shot that the needle would bear evidence of a few blood cells or skin tissue that would indicate that it had pierced human flesh, but no evidence of that fact had been present. Still, the report did verify traces of insulin, and perhaps the fatal dose had been administered through the IV, in which case, no human tissue would be expected.

More remarkable was the fact that no fingerprints or smudges had been revealed. Unreadable prints would be more usual, unless it was a gloved hand that drew the insulin and administered the dose. Still more mysterious was the unlikely location in which it was found, stuffed between the mattress and the box springs. Why would anyone stash a used needle unless it was a hasty act by someone afraid of being suddenly interrupted? Slater mused over the possibilities. He needed a breakthrough. He felt that he was on the horns of a dilemma, having very little concrete evidence that could be submitted to a grand jury. Yet, he had a nagging suspicion that Angela's death was the result of a conscious act. In his own mind, he went back and forth over the evidence, both documented and circumstantial. There were the physician's orders, the treatment records of the home nurses, and the insulin log submitted by Fornesby himself. Nothing in any of them gave a clue as to why the coroner would find high insulin levels in her blood. This was the cause of her cardiac failure. On the circumstantial side, Angela's "loving" husband had been seen in the company of another woman before and immediately after Angela's untimely death. To complicate the investigation, Barker's personal reputation and charm seemed like a layer of insulation against anyone suspecting foul play, and it was known widely that Angela was very sick. The fact remained, however, that her illnesses did not preclude the possibility of several years of fairly normal life.

His suspicions were not salved when he heard that an ex-cop named Ted Clarke had been making inquiries about the status of the investigation. Slater knew Clarke was Fornesby's chief corporate security officer. The investigation was becoming a game of cat and mouse, but it was difficult to determine which of them was the cat and which the mouse. Slater felt as though he had few allies and either had to conform to public sentiment or try something out of the ordinary to make the pot boil. Then it struck him. The idea was a bit far-fetched, but one that would never be traced to him if it didn't work out. He opened his file of business cards until he found an unpretentious one inscribed in Roman script "Elizabeth Carnaby, Dayton Daily Herald".

17

Heather Zigler was worried about her friend, Matt Fornesby. They had gone to the junior prom together and had such a good time that they had been seeing each other fairly regularly. She had noticed that Matt was somewhat preoccupied earlier in the summer, but she also knew that his mother's hospitalization was a big part of that. She tried to call him every day, and usually they'd find an excuse to meet at the Taco Bell which had been designated as the place-to-be this year. More than anything, she liked the way that they could talk about different things together. She attributed his ability to talk as a maturity born of his mother's condition. When Mrs. Fornesby died suddenly, Matt seemed to drop off the face of the planet. Heather would call during the day, but Matt didn't always answer the phone. She'd feel so frustrated when the answering machine would click on. Once she just yelled over the recording, "Matt, this is Heather, please pick up the phone!" and he did. It was then that she realized that something had to be done.

Adolescence is a crisis of trust. It takes a great sense of desperation for a teen to turn to an adult at the time in their lives where they are not sure that they are going to be treated with respect. Fortunately, there are people who quite comfortably stand as a bridge between the world of adults and the confusion of adolescent realities. When Heather tried to think whom she could confide in, the list was short. At the top was Mr. Simmons, a teacher at the high school. She and Matt had been in an environmental science class with Mr. Simmons, and they both knew that he was interested in his students, as well as his subject. On an impulse, she took a chance and called the high school. The phone rang through to the main office, and she felt rather foolish asking for a teacher when summer vacation was in progress. The secretary, however, didn't flinch. "I think he's in the building," she said. "I'll transfer you to his unit."

Heather held her breath through six rings of the phone, and breathed out when someone picked up the receiver. "Science Department," said the male voice. It was Mr. Simmons.

18

"It's good to hear your voice too," said Elizabeth Carnaby. Her mind raced back in time to when she first met Bill Slater. It was at one of the cocktail parties at a downtown hotel following the mayoral election. They were both alone at the time and seemed to gravitate toward one another. He was good-looking and bright, and they both surprised themselves by ducking out of the party to spend a quiet evening of conversation at the public cocktail lounge together making small talk. He seemed genuinely interested in her dreams of being an investigative reporter, and her frustration at paying her "dues" in the industry by taking a turn at writing about traffic accidents and filing the obituaries. The plain fact was that she was to write an account of the mayor's victory celebration, and ended up leaving with Bill before the Mayor-elect even arrived on his rounds of the evening's festivities.

The next day her report got rave reviews, especially by Bill Slater who knew the inside story. She dialed up to the party suite and talked to several friends who had stayed, then faxed in the story with her lap top computer over the hotel phone. She was nude at the time, and Slater was in bed next to her, laughing.

"Thank goodness for technology," she had said as she disconnected the temporary phone hookup.

"Does that mean we're having computer sex tonight?" he answered as he pulled her on top of him. They were both very stirred by the adventure, and forgot themselves completely. In the morning, at breakfast, they agreed to call each other, but with one thing and another, they quickly drifted back into their respective careers.

"Yes, it is very good to hear your voice, Bill," she repeated, her mind quickly returning to the present. "How can I help you?"

"I've got a bit of a mystery on my hands, and I thought you could help me solve it and get a very good story at the same time," he said.

"Oh, you need some investigative reporting?" she answered, hoping that he did not pick up on her double meanings. This was not the call she had been hoping for.

"Exactly," he answered. "It could be a very big story, but it has to be handled delicately. Ever hear of a guy named Barker Fornesby?"

19

Margaret's voice came over the intercom on Barker's desk. "Mr. Fornesby, there's a gentleman here and a young lady. They would like to talk with you about Matt. Shall I send them in?"

"I'll be right out," he answered as a flurry of questions whirled in his mind.

He stepped to his office door and opened it. Heather Zigler, Matt's girlfriend, stood before him. She was with a man he did not recognize, but the man must have read the confusion on Barker's face, for he immediately stepped forward and said, "Hi, I'm Steve Simmons, one of Matt's teachers. Heather asked me to come with her because she's worried about Matt. Can we talk now?"

"Of course," said Barker, stepping aside as Heather and Simmons stepped through his office door. He beckoned them to a casual seating area in one corner of the room. "Have a seat," he said as he settled nervously into an upholstered armchair.

Steve Simmons began to speak. "I know that you've been through a lot these past months, you and Matt, but Heather is worried that Matt isn't handling this very well. It took her a lot of courage to come to me, which tells me how deeply she's scared for him. Is that right, Heather?"

Heather nodded, somewhat overwhelmed by the situation. "Anyway," continued Simmons, "I agreed to come with her to help her talk to you. Heather, tell Matt's dad what you told me?"

"Well, Mr. Fornesby, I think you know that Matt and I are friends." Barker smiled encouragingly. "We were doing a lot of things together, as friends that is, but anyway Matt has stopped calling. I mean, not just me, he's just kind of dropped out of everything. Nobody has seen him, and he doesn't even answer the phone."

"I call him during the day," responded Barker, "and when he doesn't answer, I just figure he's out with his friends, and I know he's not mad at you."

"I hope not," said Heather, relaxing a little. "But he's not out with anyone. That's why I went to see Mr. Simmons, and he said that you ought to know this. There are a whole lot of kids who'd like to help him, but... I just hope that he's talking to somebody."

"I've got to admit that I've been pretty preoccupied. I can't tell you what Matt is thinking, but I appreciate that you've come to me. Matt is very lucky to have friends like you. I guess that makes me lucky, too. Do you two have any ideas about what I can do?"

"Well, we're here to give support," offered Steve Simmons, "but I think it may be deeper than we can handle. I know that you go to the Presbyterian Church. Davis McGowan has a pretty good reputation among the kids, and I think that Matt would trust him. At least that would be a place to start. I'd guess he knows what you've been going through."

"Funny, I called on him when Matt's mother died, but didn't think of him just now. You're right, though. I think he'd know where we could start anyway. Maybe it needs to start with me. I've not been able to talk with Matt much at all. He's so much like his mother, or at least, he reminds me of her."

"But you need to do something now," blurted Heather.

"I will, Heather. I promise." A look of relief came over Heather's youthful face and she smiled at Steve Simmons. The two rose from their seats, and they each shook hands with Barker before leaving the office.

20

Davis McGowan could hardly remember his two weeks on the boat as he sorted through the unopened mail and the telephone messages. In his mind, he sorted them into three piles, urgent, not so urgent, and crap. The urgent stack included a premature baby in the neonatal unit of the hospital. The not so urgent was a request for a wedding a year from next October, and among the crap was an irate member who was threatening to withhold all contributions if the rumor regarding the new carpet in the lounge was true. That was the most draining part of his work. Life and death issues had a sense of reality, but the rantings of the perpetually miserable carried no life and little hope. Yet, these were the people that he had pledged to serve, and he always felt a sense of remorse that he could not bring them to see that there were issues of life larger than money and color swatches. He was in a cynical mood, and invited the associate pastor into his office as she walked by.

"What do you think, Linda?" he asked. "Is it too unpastoral if I suggest that they put their money where the 'sun don't shine' and no one will ever try to get it again?"

"I bet I know who you're talking about," was the answer.

"Yep, the children are throwing tantrums again. You know, I wish they would stop giving to the church. Then they'd lose all their weapons, and just maybe they'd find out how empty they are! Oh well, it's really nice to be back!" They both laughed.

"Actually, it is nice to have you back. Sometimes it's crazy around here, and when you're not around, they ask for me!" Davis and Linda got along very well. They trusted each other's professional ability and respected each other's dedication. It was a very good combination.

"Thanks," was his only response.

"Davis," a voice came over the speaker phone. "Barker Fornesby is on line one for you."

"I'll bet you five dollars that this conversation won't be trivial," said Davis.

"That's a bet that I will not accept," said the other pastor. "Barker Fornesby is not a trivial person." She stepped out of the office, closing the door behind her.

21

"It's good to see you, too," said Bill Slater responding to Elizabeth Carnaby' s greeting. He had stood when he saw her enter the restaurant. They hugged politely and took seats opposite each other in the dimly lit restaurant.

"I haven't eaten at the King Cole for a long time," said Elizabeth, breaking the silence.

"Nor have I," stated Slater. "It's outside my normal operating budget."

"I'm glad," chuckled Elizabeth, "I'd have to write an investigative report on where our public officials are getting their lunch money!" The two smiled at each other for the first time.

"Well," said Slater, "this is a special occasion."

"Oh?" retorted Carnaby. "Are we having an anniversary that I didn't know about?" The words were no sooner out of her mouth than she wished they hadn't been spoken. They represented what she was feeling, but she had promised herself that she would keep an open mind.

"No, nothing like that," blushed Slater. "I'm sorry that we couldn't work something out, but I guess other things got in the way."

"Like two careers going in different directions?" responded Elizabeth.

"Something like that," Slater offered. "Anyway, what I wanted to talk about relates to our two careers rather than us. How about if I tell you the whole story, we have a nice lunch, and we start over on us?"

"Okay, I'm game," offered Elizabeth raising her water glass. "Here's to a truce, and maybe a lasting peace." Slater joined her in the toast. "Now what's all this about Barker Fornesby?" she asked.

"Do you know much about him?" asked Slater.

"Not really. After your call I began to do research. He was brought in as a *Wunderkind* at Data Specialties, Inc. All the indicators say he's not been a disappointment. He's well-liked, resourceful, and in line for bigger and better things. There are even rumors that headhunters have been after him for years, but Data Specialties makes it worth his while to stay."

"For not knowing much, you know a lot," winked Slater. "Did you know that his wife died recently?"

"Yes, her obit is listed in his personal file down at the paper. We keep an active file on community hot-shots. Wanna know what's in your record?" she said with twinkle in her eye.

"Hmm," responded Slater, "maybe I don't what to know that. It might be too personal, and we have a truce, right?"

"Right! And it's not bad at all, but I've changed the subject. Go on," she encouraged.

"Everything you've said about Fornesby is true," continued Slater. "He's well-connected in this town, and so what's *not* being said is as significant as the information in your database. The paper did not report the cause of Angela Fornesby's death. It merely stated that she suffered from a terminal illness, and contributions were directed to the cancer and diabetes societies."

"You mean, she didn't die of natural causes?" asked Carnaby.

"No, she didn't! That's the one thing we do know. Her heart failure was directly due to an overdose of insulin. The mystery centers around how it happened. We've gone over the family's record of glucose levels and dosages. We've matched that with the visiting home nurse's record of insulin administered through the IV and can't find an explanation."

"And you suspect Fornesby?" queried the journalist.

Slater hesitated. "He seems the logical choice, particularly when we found out that he has a 'friend' on the side. She's a nurse who works at the hospital."

"The plot thickens," added Carnaby.

"Think about it, Elizabeth. The murder of the terminally ill is an almost undetectable crime. I say 'almost' because we've detected this one. The strange thing is that no one wants to see it! You've got a well-connected widower as a suspect, and everyone wants to show sympathy."

"But aren't you overlooking other possibilities?" Elizabeth continued. "What about an accident, or maybe suicide? If she was terminally ill, why couldn't he and this nurse just lay low? Wouldn't it just be a matter of time?"

"I think that we ruled out the accident theory by checking the injection record," argued Slater. "As for suicide, everyone we spoke to said that Mrs. Fornesby had a positive attitude toward her treatment. As for waiting, it probably would have been a matter of years, not weeks or months. There's also a financial consideration. Even with good insurance, I'm sure Fornesby would have to put out a bundle while he was waiting."

"Everything you say makes sense," responded Carnaby.

"But that's not all!" offered Slater. "Barker Fornesby is hiding something. I told you that everyone seems like they are making sympathetic excuses rather than looking at the facts. Well, he's got his chief of security, a man named

Ted Clarke, making discrete inquiries about the whole investigation."

"Are you sure?"

"Yes! When a former cop starts asking questions, people notice. And, I don't think it's an accident that the guy reports directly to Fornesby. Security is one of his departments."

"Okay," said Elizabeth, "I'm following you, but why are you calling? No, let me guess. You have suddenly remembered the power of the press."

"Something like that," continued Slater. "It just seems to me that if there's any hope of making the pot boil, we have to turn up the heat."

"I noticed that you said, 'we'," answered Carnaby. "Does that mean a partnership?"

"Not so anyone would notice," responded Slater. "In fact, we never had this discussion! I just thought that you could convince your editor that a series of articles on euthanasia might be interesting to your readers. You could interview a few key people on the subject."

"Like you," inserted Carnaby.

"Yes, like me," agreed Slater, "and like a certain intensive care nurse. I think that Fornesby might squirm a little and push hard enough to make a grand jury take notice. But this would only be if you think it's a good idea. I'd never want to be accused of influencing an investigation." Slater winked and flashed a smile.

"Does this mean that we will have to wear trench coats and meet late at night in parking garages?" said Elizabeth pushing the conversation to a lighter note. Slater laughed, but a certain nervousness crept into his voice. The conversation had begun to shift from attorney and journalist to man and woman.

"It probably wouldn't be too smart to be seen together too much," said Slater, trying to recover. "At least not in the short term. If anything came of this investigation, I wouldn't want to give the defense a secret weapon." His response made sense, but also provided an easy dodge to a rather open-ended subject.

"Let me put it this way," added Slater, "wouldn't it be very timely for you if an indictment of a public figure like Barker Fornesby came down just as you were finishing a series on mercy killing?" He had made his point while managing to keep himself walled off from her scrutiny.

"Okay," responded Carnaby. "I'll present an idea for a series, but I can't promise you anything. It will be a series written the way I want it."

"Fair enough," concluded Slater. "Now it's my turn to propose a toast," he said, lifting his glass in the manner that she had earlier. "To us, working together."

"But not being together," she added. Slater looked at his watch.

22

When Davis McGowan pulled into the Fornesby drive, he knew that he was playing a long shot. He had called the house earlier in hopes that Matt would answer the phone, but the answering machine had picked up the call. In their brief conversation, Barker had warned him that Matt was living the life of a recluse, and that he had been tipped off by a visit from Matt's girlfriend and a teacher from school.

He slammed the car door hard, hoping that his presence would make Matt look out the window. His relationship with the young man had always been friendly. He was a perceptive teenager, and had made the confirmation class a joy the year that he was in the eighth grade. Most eighth graders sit through class with blank stares daring the teacher to say anything new or interesting. Matt was one of those naturally curious people who wanted to know why and who and how about everything. He seemed fascinated by archaeology and textual criticism. The temptation was to structure the class for Matt and to forget the yawns and eye-rolls of his classmates when he asked a question. Ever since that time, Matt and Davis had a mutual respect for each other. Davis hoped that their personal history would bring Matt to the door rather than force him into the deeper recesses of the house. It worked. When he rang the doorbell, the door opened, and a pallid youth let him enter.

Once inside the house, Davis could further appreciate the contrast between the youth and his former self. His friends had done well to blow the whistle on Matt's solitude.

"Hi, Matt," Davis said as nonchalantly as possible. "I thought you might like to talk."

The simple statement opened the flood gates, as the usually poised young man started to talk about everything at once. He rambled for a quarter of an hour about his mother, his promises to God, and his inability to talk to his father. At times his voice failed him when his throat swelled to choke his speech. In the end, he put his head in his hands and cried. Davis sat by quietly. Some of what he was hearing made no sense at all, but it did not matter what he understood, only that Matt was finally talking. When the words began to slow and the pauses extended into deep silence, Davis rose to his feet and went to the kitchen. He filled a glass of water and took a tissue from the dispenser on the counter. "Here," he said handing Matt the tissue and setting the glass in front of him. "It sounds like you've been alone in this dark place a long time."

Matt shook his head slowly. "Yes, it has been a long time. I keep going around in circles, and I can't stop. Am I crazy, Dr. McGowan?"

"Crazy?" answered Davis. "You are one of the sanest people I know. It's the world that's gone crazy around you."

A long silence was followed by a desperately whispered confession. "That night, the night Mom died, I promised God that I'd take care of her, but I think that I killed her!"

"Now that is crazy!" interjected Davis. "How did you kill your mother?"

The intensity of Davis' response caught Matt off guard and snapped him out of his panic. "Well, she died of an insulin overdose, and I gave her that injection just after the nurse left, and that's what killed her. Will they arrest me?"

94

"Nobody's going to arrest you, Matt. Even if what you said is true, it would have been a terrible, terrible accident. Unless, you meant to do it? Did you?"

"Never!" bristled Matt, and Davis was pleased that the strong character of the young man still lived within his weakened form.

"Of course you wouldn't," said Davis. "That's the whole point."

"Then did God do it?" Davis' mind reeled at the turn of the conversation.

"I can't tell you what happened," he answered, "and maybe we'll never know, but I can tell you this: God didn't want your mother dead, and you didn't either. It is something that happened to you and to everyone who loved her, but it's not your fault. Suppose something for me. Suppose your mother could come back here for five minutes and sit here with us, what do you think she'd say?"

A long silence enveloped them and tears ran down Matt's cheeks as his squeaking voice spoke the sacred words, "'Never worry about me. I'm so proud of my son and my husband.' That's what I think she'd say. That's what she said to me when I gave her the insulin."

"And what would you say to her?" Davis asked.

"I'd say, 'I'm sorry, I love you Mom! More than anything.'"

"Matt, what would you be sorry for? That you love her?"

"No, not for that, but for everything else. The time I got drunk and the time I threw the keys at the wall," he said, gesturing to the unpainted repair on the drywall. "I'd never be sorry for loving her."

"And do you think that she'd stopped loving you when you got drunk or threw the keys?"

"I guess not," said Matt.

"I don't have to guess, Matt. She'd never stop loving you, or your father. Have you talked to him? He cares, you know."

"I guess so, but he's busy, and it was always easier to talk with Mom."

"I'll bet he finds it just as hard to talk with you. Suppose I could arrange an outing... somewhere away from here. How about if we go fossil hunting at Caesar Creek? We could talk as much or as little as you want, and I'll get your Dad to come, too."

"He won't do that."

"Oh, yeah? Just you wait." Davis went to the kitchen phone and looked in his pocket calendar for the hastily written phone number of Barker's office. He punched in the numbers, and stood waiting until a male voice answered. "Barker, this is Davis McGowan. I'm with Matt right now, and we'd like to invite you to go fossil hunting with us on Friday. Can you clear your day?" A broad smile crossed his face as he turned to Matt with a wink. "Good, I'll drive and pick the two of you up at the house at 9:00. See you on Friday." He returned the phone to its cradle. "It's all set."

"You knew he'd do that, didn't you?" retorted Matt.

"Well, I had asked him to clear Friday if he could. You see, Matt, he wants to talk, too, but doesn't know how. Maybe Friday will be different for you both." The two shook hands, then hugged.

"Thank you, Dr. McGowan. For everything."

"Sure, Matt, just don't forget to get your Dad ready for Friday. He probably doesn't know a thing about trilobites." The last comment brought a smile to Matt's face, and it was the last thing that Davis saw as he left the house.

23

Deb Walker looked up from her paperwork when she heard her name spoken from the front of the nurses' station. The records clerk seemed to be directing someone to her. She had almost completed the day's work and was finishing the notations on a chart. It was a particularly sad situation, a seventeen year old young man with a head injury from a motorcycle accident. He hadn't been wearing a helmet, and today was the beginning of the fourth week of his coma.

His father had given him the sport bike as an early graduation present, much to the distress of his estranged wife, the boy's mother. While they each took turns at the bedside, the blame and guilt could fill all four floors of the hospital's west wing. Deb sighed as she closed the chart, and an approaching woman quickly called her back to reality.

"Hello, I'm Elizabeth Carnaby," said a slender young brunette in a tailored suit. "I'm a writer for the Dayton Daily Herald. I'm writing a series of articles on families in crisis with a critically or terminally ill family member. I was given your name as someone who could give me a nurse's perspective."

Deb could not imagine who would have given her name to anyone, much less a reporter. As to families in crisis, her thoughts jumped back to the comatose youth in the glass-walled room nearby. "I don't know what I can tell you," answered Deb, "but I will be glad to talk."

"I came now because I found out that you were ending your shift. Are you finished? I'll be glad to wait if you're not."

"You are a reporter if you know when my shift ends," laughed Deb. "And I am finished. Just now, in fact, and glad to get out of here."

"There's a restaurant around the corner, DiCarlo's. I'd be glad to buy you dinner or a drink," invited Elizabeth.

"A glass of wine sounds good, but I'll pass on the dinner," answered Deb.

The two walked down corridors familiar to Deb who took each turn with an automatic precision, while Elizabeth, in contrast, took in every detail of hospital life. There were patients walking gingerly with a nurse on one arm and an IV pole trailing behind.

"Does any of this ever get to you?" asked Elizabeth after a bit.

"Any of what?" questioned Deb.

"The tubes and the pain and the long faces."

"Oh, that," said Deb, "you have to learn to look beyond the obvious. These people aren't sick; they're getting well. A lot of what you see is determined by what you think is there. I'm a nurse, and I choose to see that they are people getting well, rather than people in pain. It's just that pain is sometimes the cost of getting well, that's all."

Elizabeth was struck by the clarity of Deb's answer. This was a perceptive person who had thought through many of life's issues. She was one of those people who would never be noticed as an authority on anything, and yet was a storehouse of practical wisdom. Bill Slater's description had made Deb sound like a seductress rather than this soft-spoken, thoughtful woman who was obviously at the end of a long day. While this interview didn't seem a likely source of sinister information, it would be useful in the real article that had been promised to an editor.

* * *

Two glasses of white zinfandel were served very quickly after they took their seats in the cocktail lounge. They engaged in light conversation before Elizabeth posed the first serious question to Deb. "You said earlier that you choose to see people as getting well rather than as being sick. What if they aren't 'getting well'?"

"Sometimes you can't even tell," answered Deb, "but before we start, can I ask one thing?"

"Sure," said Elizabeth.

"If we're going to talk openly, I have to be sure about what you're going to write. I mean, I'm talking to you and I don't even know you. It's difficult for me to talk about these subjects without talking about people who have been my patients. They deserve confidentiality, and I don't know what you're going to write."

"Don't worry," said Elizabeth assuringly. "This is really an article about nurses' attitudes, not patient records. If I need to refer to a specific example, I promise that I will make it generic enough not to be recognizable."

"Okay," said Deb haltingly. "Right now I've got a kid in a coma, and two parents who can't handle it. They want to know if he's getting better. You can't blame them. I've got a daughter nearly that age. If I were in their place, I'd want to know anything that sounded vaguely hopeful. So I tell them that I want to believe that he's getting better. A coma can be a body's way of shutting down for healing, but then a week turns into two and then three. I don't know if he's getting better, or dying slowly, one brain cell at a time."

"But the parents want to stay positive, so you do too, right?"

"That's part of it, but it's not just for them. Who knows if a person is getting well or not? The doctors think that they know, but they're just guessing. I've seen docs who give up on a comatose patient, only to have the person open their eyes and say, 'I'm starving, what's for dinner?'" The two women laughed together.

"But that doesn't happen often, does it?" asked Elizabeth.

"No, but when somebody you love is lying there, you want to believe that it will happen *this time*."

"So you hold it out for the family to latch onto."

"Not exactly. The family holds it out for us. And, well, it isn't our job to pull the rug out from under them at the time they are most vulnerable. Sometimes, that's what we have to do though. We have to begin bringing reality into their thinking, and we hope to God we're wrong. Face it, even in the 'miracle cases' things are not the way they are envisioned. People think that the person is going to jump out of bed and be their old self. Most never become their *old selves*. They have years of physical therapy or brain damage or memory loss. That's one of the most difficult things for the family. They get robbed of the past. The person can't remember the sunset they all shared when they went to the mountains, or even the names of the people in the family album."

"Do you think some families would think of euthanasia, mercy killing, as a way out?" asked Elizabeth moving closer to the point.

"No, I don't think so. Not at first anyway," answered Deb thoughtfully. "You've got to remember that I'm a trauma nurse. Mostly I see people who are victims of accidents, rather than those who have a terminal diagnosis."

"And you think there's a difference?" responded Elizabeth quickly.

"Oh yes, definitely. First there's the shock that the family has to deal with. They want to believe that everything is under control and that it's just a matter of time and treatment. Even when there's obviously extensive brain damage, they haven't the background to understand what that means. I think the idea of mercy killing comes later in trauma cases. The family looks back to the night of the injury and says, 'It would have been better if they hadn't made it to the hospital.'"

"But what about families that decide to 'pull the plug'?"

"That's not euthanasia. That's letting nature take its course and allowing the person to die. There comes a point where you have to decide whether you are prolonging life or prolonging the dying process. If there's no reasonable hope that putting a person on a machine will give their body time to recover, then there has to be a more compelling reason than to just maintain body functions on a corpse. Pardon my bluntness," added Deb.

"No problem, I appreciate your openness," commented Elizabeth. "In fact, I'm struck by how much thought you've given to this."

"If you haven't worked it out in your brain, you wouldn't last long in a trauma unit. You have to believe that there are worse things than dying, and after a few weeks, every new trauma nurse knows that."

"You mentioned something about 'a more compelling reason' to put a person on a machine. If you know that you can't save their life, what could be a reason for doing that?"

"Sometimes the family insists on it and what you are doing is buying time for them to get some psychological perspective. Sometimes another life is at stake, like a woman who's pretty far along in a pregnancy and is brain dead, but the unborn child is still viable if it can be supported *in utero*. Even then, sometimes I wonder. It's like we believe that when we can do something we have to try, but there's a fuzzy line that is easy to cross, and the superhuman effort becomes a cruelty. Like I said, you have to believe that there are worse things than dying."

"You mentioned that you are a trauma nurse. How would it be different if I spoke to a nurse who works with the terminally ill?"

"I'm sure it would be different if you were to talk with a hospice nurse. I'd only be guessing, but I would think that the issues would appear very differently to the family and the patient. When we disconnect the machines, we allow nature to take its course believing that it will be less painful and with more dignity. Euthanasia is specifically not allowing nature to take its course because that would be the more painful course of action."

"You sound like you aren't opposed to the possibility of mercy killing?" added Elizabeth.

"I guess I don't know what I think." answered Deb. "It probably depends on the people and on the circumstance."

Elizabeth zeroed in on this last opening and asked the question that Bill Slater wanted addressed. "What about someone like Angela Fornesby? I know you knew her and her condition."

Deb blanched at the sudden mention of Angela's name. She did not fully understand the source of the question and didn't know whether to be suspicious or candid. Perhaps Elizabeth was a friend of Barker's. On the other hand, she had not mentioned his name. "I didn't know Angela Fornesby at all. I know Barker slightly through an internet blog, and so that's why I attended the funeral. I really haven't had much of a chance to talk with him since then, so I'm not of much help. Gosh, I've got to run. My daughter will be waiting for dinner."

"Thank you for your help," Elizabeth called after her, but Deb was already near the door. Deb had no idea what had just happened, or why she had lied about not talking with Barker. The two had been in daily contact over the computer, and had even gone out for dinner. It was at that time that Barker had passed on some information to her, and now her knowledge seemed like a burden. She had sworn herself to secrecy that night, and they were both sure that they weren't observed. Now, however, someone else was raising questions.

24

"Mr. Fornesby," Margaret's voice came over the intercom.

"Yes, Margaret," answered Barker who was seated at his desk.

"Mr. Fornesby, Mr. Clarke from security is here to see you."

"Send him right in, Margaret," answered Barker, sitting up quickly. The door opened and Ted Clarke entered.

"You're wearing your police officer face, Ted," began Barker. "Bad news?"

"Might be, Barker, you'll have to decide. Anyway, I didn't want to say this over the phone."

"Now you've got me scared. Spit it out, Chief," said Barker as lightly as he could, but there was a growing hesitancy within him.

"It's Bill Slater. There are real mixed feelings about that guy. Some think he might want to take a run at politics, and he needs a case that will bring him into the public eye. My guess is that he's fishing for a big one, and you might be the one he wants to land."

"What in the world are you talking about?"

"Only that he's sending a whole file to the grand jury. He says that it doesn't add up, Angela's death, that is. He wants an indictment, and rumor has it that he's even going to suggest first degree murder."

"That's a crock! The guy must be crazy! Who would believe that for a minute? Who would even want to kill Angela?" Barker had not been prepared for this news.

"Well, it hasn't happened yet," consoled Ted Clarke. "It's more like an idea he's floating around. Let's hope some jurors will have more sense than to issue indictments where there has been no evidence of a crime. The danger is that an ambitious politician might be able to get just as much out of a story about 'the one that got away' as easily as about the one that's been stuffed and mounted. Sorry, about all the 'fish talk', boss, but that's where I'm headed-- up to Lake Erie. Four of us are chartering a boat out of Huron for a little fishing tomorrow."

"I would never have guessed, Ted," smiled Barker. "Thanks for staying on top of this. You've been a good friend, and I just hope that Bill Slater doesn't have anybody on his grand jury who will take the bait and believe his lies."

"Nah, don't worry about that. All us fishermen are liars, but we know it. You got to watch out for the liars who don't know it. I'll keep my ears and eyes open."

"Thanks, Ted. I don't know what I can do against the rumor mill. I'll just stay close to home and be a good boy. Right?"

"Just sit tight. I'm sure that I can give you some notice as to what's going to come out of the grand jury. In fact, two of my best sources will be a boat with me tomorrow," Ted Clarke said with a smile.

"So this fishing is all in the line of duty?"

"Just doing my job, Boss!"

"Well," added Barker, "I hope your duty gets you a string of walleye!"

"I'll bring some back for you!"

Ted Clark was out the door, and Barker was alone with his thoughts. The lighthearted jibes of a moment earlier drained from him as he sank silently into his chair.

25

Caesar Creek Lake is a man-made reservoir to help prevent flooding in the Ohio River Valley. The project converted area farm fields into lake bottom and a recreational lake for fishing and boating. During the course of plowing out a spillway, bulldozers cut through a wall of sedimentary rock that proved to be fossil rich, and the Army Corp of Engineers ended up managing fossil hunters, in addition to water levels.

Davis McGowan knew the procedure from previous outings. Matt, Barker, and he would have to register at the visitor center as fossil collectors, and be given the guidelines regarding the retrieval of specimens. As they turned off Route 73 toward the center, Davis began to explain what they would soon find. Matt had been here before, but Barker was completely in the dark with regard to what he could expect.

"What if we can't find any fossils?" he asked.

"Don't worry, Dad, we'll find plenty. It's the trilobites that are tough to find, but we'll be up to our ears in brachiopods," chimed in Matt.

"Are you speaking English?" bantered his father. Barker was not used to being out of control, but he was crossing into an area of expertise that was far removed from his experience. Give him a balance sheet or a strategic planning report, and Barker could take charge in a minute, but brachiopods and trilobites were not on his MBA vocabulary list.

"What Matt is saying," offered Davis, "is that we'll find fossils. This place is so full of them, you'll trip over them. The common ones are like little sea shells, those are the brachiopods, but there are rarer ones like the trilobites. We're going to test your powers of observation, aren't we Matt?" He glanced in the rear view mirror to make eye contact with Matt who was seated in the back seat.

"Once this area was covered by sea water," offered Matt. "That was the Ordovician Period, when the animals lived here."

Barker turned from his position in the passenger's seat to face his son. "Where was I when my son became an expert on prehistoric sea life?" Matt blushed.

"Matt knows a good many things, Barker," interrupted Davis. "That's one of the reasons for this outing. I thought it would be better for you to meet here at Matt's 'office' rather than your own, and here we are." He steered his car into the visitor center's parking area.

The three of them entered the cedar-sided building. While Davis registered with the ranger, Matt showed his father the displays, and Barker seemed genuinely curious, if not about the displays, at least about his son's familiarity with the geological history of the place. Davis did not hurry to interrupt, but lingered around a display of the hydraulics related to the construction of the reservoir until Matt and Barker seemed to notice his absence.

"Are we ready?" asked Barker.

"All set," said Davis. "We're legal to collect small fossils as long as we don't use tools or dig." Barker didn't ask for an explanation; he was along for the ride and would let others lead the way. "Here, you might want to look at this," said Davis handing a brochure to Barker. It was entitled "Common Fossils of Caesar Creek Lake".

When they returned to the car, both Matt and Barker settled in the back seat and the son was explaining fossil recognition. Davis was pleased. He had hoped that this could be a day of bridge building between father and son, and it seemed that Barker was on the way toward making the discovery that most parents want, but fail to recognize, that their child has become a capable adult.

The spillway at Caesar Creek runs for about a mile and is a flat-bottomed trench a quarter of a mile wide. At the Eastern edge of the trench are shale cliffs cut open to reveal their fossilized treasures. The three men slowly walked toward the ridge, and Matt and Davis were amused by Barker's reaction. Having worried about not finding fossils, he soon had his hands full of specimens.

"We told you that you'd trip over them," said Davis, winking at Matt.

Matt, however, was as excited as his father. He was excited to show him the types of fossils, and carefully explained the differences between the brachiopods and the gastropods. They also found fragments of the "sea lily" or crinoid. Finally, Barker could stand it no longer, but asked the question on his mind. "How do you know so much? You must have come here often, Matt."

Matt grew suddenly silent. "I did, with Mom. It was our place. When I was in Junior High, we'd come here whenever you went on a business trip. We always wanted to find a trilobite, but never did."

"I'm sorry, I must have forgotten that. You really miss her, don't you?" Matt's voice failed him and he nodded. "I do too, son, more than you can imagine."

"Everything I see hurts because it reminds me of her," said Matt choking back the tears.

"I know," said Barker, "I guess that's why I've been staying at work so much. It's hard to be in the house or do the things we used to do."

"When Mom died, it's like the family died," observed Matt.

"Only if we let it. I guess we have to learn to be a new kind of family, and if we don't, I'd think we'd be kind of letting your mother down." They both stood silently for a long time. They had not realized that Davis had wandered off and was watching them from a distance. He could not tell what they were saying, but he saw them hug. So much of love is finding time and space, and here on the ocean bed of the Ordovician Sea two generations met, at least for a moment.

26

Barker was seated at the breakfast table drinking the last of his coffee when the phone rang. For him 8:00 was a rather late start on the day, but early for the phone to ring. It was Deb Walker, who seemed distressed.

"Barker, I'm glad to find you at home," she said.

"I'm waiting until after Matt's up before I leave for work these days. What's wrong? You sound anxious."

"Barker, I am so sorry. Have you seen the paper this morning?"

"Yes, I'm reading it now, but I haven't noticed anything," he said.

"Look at the 'Metro' section in the little box labeled 'Next Week in the News'."

Barker turned to the center section of the paper and found the notice that troubled Deb. It read: "Next week, Elizabeth Carnaby presents a series of interviews entitled 'Euthanasia: Mercy or Murder?' On Monday, she interviews William Slater from the Prosecutor's Office who says, 'The murder of the terminally ill is a difficult crime to detect.' Others in the series will include interviews with health care providers."

"Barker, she came to me and asked about you and Angie."

"What?" questioned Barker in disbelief.

"Three days ago, Elizabeth Carnaby came to my station at work to talk about dealing with trauma victims and the terminally ill. All of a sudden, she asked about Angie and what you two were thinking in the days before her death."

"You didn't tell her anything, did you?"

"Of course not! I just got out of there as quickly as I could. I told her that I didn't know Angie and she'd have to talk to you. Both those things are true, but I certainly wouldn't tell her anything else; I gave you my word."

"Sorry, if I sounded like I doubted you, Deb. I'm sure you did fine. I think all this is Bill Slater's fishing expedition."

"What's that?" inquired Deb.

"Nothing, I'm just thinking out loud," replied Barker. "Don't worry; it will be okay, but thanks for calling. I'll let you know if anything comes of this."

The two hung up the phones, and Barker quickly pulled his things together and left for his office.

27

Barker was preoccupied when he walked into the outer office past Margaret's desk.

"Barker," she called to him, "Ted Clarke is waiting for you in your office. I told him that you weren't in yet, but he insisted on waiting."

"That's fine, Margaret. I wanted to see him, too." The expression on Margaret's face turned to curiosity. She had seen Barker's many moods over the years, but all of a sudden he was showing her something that she had never seen before. If she could have named it, it might have been 'panic', but she didn't, except to note that something terrible had or was about to happen. Without another word, Barker threw open the door to his private office. Ted Clarke stood quickly, partly from force of habit, partly because of the sharpness of Barker's actions.

"I take it that you've seen the paper, Ted," Barker began.

"Yes, I did. A lot of people saw it, and there's a group of folk at city hall who are pissed about it," answered Clarke.

"How so?"

"Well, they see Slater's hand in all of this, but he's claiming his innocence. He says he was approached by a reporter with some theoretical questions, but everyone remembers that there were rumors about those two a year or so ago."

"Rumors?" queried Barker.

"Rumors that they were a little friendlier with each other than reporter and prosecutor, if you take my meaning."

"What meaning are they taking downtown?"

"Most think he's making a play for the grand jury. He'll make the big disclaimer in the paper that he can't comment on any current cases before the grand jury, but I know he's going to lay a file in front of them and ask them to give serious consideration to a situation that could have been murder."

"Do I have to guess whose name is on that file?" asked Barker.

"No, Boss, you don't have to guess. The thing is full of circumstantial stuff including a dinner meeting with a woman named Deb Walker who, quite by coincidence, is going to be quoted in a newspaper article this week, if I'm not mistaken."

"Oh, shit!" exclaimed Barker. Ted was surprised to hear an expletive coming out of Barker's mouth. "Will anyone buy the stuff?" continued Fornesby.

"Who knows?" came the reply. "If the grand jury feels jerked around, it could backfire big time. Sometimes they're pretty independent and they don't take the antics of the would-be politicians very well. On the other hand, everyone likes a good scandal and the trial would be a juicy one."

"I don't want a trial," stated Barker. "I don't even want an open hearing. Got any ideas, Ted?"

"Well, have you got any friends at the Herald? I mean, Deb Walker's name hasn't been put in print yet.

That name would be the most damaging link in the minds of the grand jury. They'll see that name when they open your file. You don't want any of them to have read it in the newspaper the week before."

"I see what you mean, Ted. I guess I have my work cut out. I was hoping that all this would just blow over. I think Matt and I have been through enough."

"That's what you get for being 'Barker Fornesby, the up-and-coming VP'! Ever think of becoming a lowly security guard like me?"

"Do lowly security guards ever visit people in jail?"

"It won't come to that, Boss, just hang in there."

* * *

Ted Clarke's words didn't give much encouragement to Barker Fornesby whose hand was shaking when he picked up his phone to tell Margaret to get Elizabeth Carnaby on the phone. Before he could hit the intercom code, he thought better of having a secretary dial the number, and rummaged through his desk drawer until he found a phone directory.

28

The Great Miami River cuts a path through Dayton on its way toward joining the Ohio River to the south. Residents of southwestern Ohio are offended by outsiders who wonder at the frequency of the word "Miami" in the names of companies and businesses. But the word has a long history beginning with the Miami Nation of Native Americans who first settled in the Valley. The Miami

University in Oxford was the home of McGuffy and his famous *Reader*, and still takes pride in the slogan "Miami was a university before Florida was a state."

Along the river corridor is the Carillon Park, with its reconstructed historic buildings and quiet walkways. The bicycle shop of two famous Daytonians, Wilbur and Orville, is there along with the Deeds Carillon that chimes out the quarter hour from its grassy hillock. Barker Fornesby walked slowly up that knoll. He was thinking about the meeting that was about to take place, and how much of his future could hinge on the next few minutes. He stepped up onto the stone dais that formed a circular walkway around the carillon tower. A woman was waiting there.

"Elizabeth Carnaby?" he said. She turned toward him with a look that told him she was studying him. "I'm Barker Fornesby," he offered.

"I know," she said, "I checked your photo in our file at the Herald. It's good to meet you." She offered her hand in a cordial handshake.

"Frankly, Ms. Carnaby, I don't know how to begin this conversation. I'm a pretty direct person, and not very good at role play, so can I just level with you?"

"That might be your best bet," she said coolly.

"Okay," he said with a pause, "then it's just the facts, Ma'am!" Her look softened slightly. "I don't really know what is going on, but I know you talked to Deb Walker and specifically asked about me. I also know that Bill Slater is in on this and he's got some notion that Deb and I have something going on between us. Other than friendship, that is."

"So far, I'm with you," answered Elizabeth.

"I could also tell you that Deb and I are just friends and primarily share electronic mail over the computer, but you'll believe whatever you want, and society doesn't believe that men and women can be friends without having sex. The plain fact is, however, that we are just that: friends. She was a sympathetic ear when Angie was sick, but like I said, you will believe what you want."

Barker could not read the effects of his words on Elizabeth, so he just continued. "She told me that you were curious about what went on in families of people who are terminally ill before you dropped my name, and I see that your article is about euthanasia. There are some who would like to make Angie's death a murder or a suicide or something, and quite honestly, I can't tell you what happened. But I can tell you what I felt and feel, and that is my best hope at not being tried in the press for something I did not do.

"You want to know what people feel when they get a diagnosis. I can tell you what I felt. I felt everything and I felt nothing. I'd go from being flooded with emotion and the memory of every kindness, every vacation, every move that we made together. I'd remember the girl I fell in love with in college, and I'd want to hold her. Then I'd feel numbness like none of it was true. It couldn't be true because we still had dreams, but the visits to the hospital and the lab tests were all true. And I thought about raising

116

a son I hardly knew because I had been so busy with a career that suddenly seemed trivial."

Barker's words came quickly and with an emotional force that surprised even him. It caught Elizabeth off guard, for she had imagined this man to be tough and hard-driving, but he seemed suddenly vulnerable. As a reporter, she was always ready with a question, but all that followed was a long silence until at last Barker spoke again.

"Angie and I had a lot of hope, but we also knew that it would be rough. Even before the cancer, we knew that her diabetes could, over the long haul, lead to blindness and circulatory problems. Sometimes she'd have nightmares about having her legs amputated. Sometimes we'd have to laugh at ourselves because there was no basis for any long-term hope except that our love wanted to make it so. Does any of this make sense to you?"

Elizabeth wanted to take his hand, but instead, just managed a few words, "Yes, it does."

"I'm doing the best I can for my son. I can't bring back his mother. I really don't understand what the fuss is about Angie's death. We're the ones, Matt and I, who feel the pain, but evidently somebody is not through with us yet. Do you know why I asked to meet you here? I mean, at this place, the carillon?"

The sudden question startled Elizabeth. "Not really," said Elizabeth, "I assumed it was because it was close to your office."

"No," said Barker. "It is because I have walked here a lot over the years and never knew the meaning of that," he said, pointing to the bronze-work on the door to the carillon tower. In the grill work was a portion of a poem by Longfellow:

> It was as if an earthquake
> rent the hearthstones of a continent
> and made forlorn the households
> born of peace on earth,
> good will to men.

> And in despair I bowed my head,
> "There is no peace on earth," I said,
> for hate is strong and mocks the song
> of peace on earth,
> good will to men.

> Then pealed the bells more loud and deep
> God is not dead, nor does he sleep.
> The wrong shall fail, the right prevail
> with peace on earth,
> good will to men.

"The language is sexist, but I know what he felt," said Barker. "My house, my family have been shaken, but I will fight to make it well again. I owe it to Matt and to myself and to the memory of a woman I still love very much."

"You are a surprising man, Barker Fornesby," said Elizabeth at last. "I came here to string you out and discover justice, but now I don't know who you are at all. You are either a victim or a great role player in spite of what you may have said up-front, and yet, I feel that you are neither."

* * *

That night, Elizabeth Carnaby sat at her word processor and pondered the revisions of her euthanasia series. All the theories about truth in journalism served no useful purpose. Whose truth would she write? Did it matter? She stared at the monitor, until her hands took their place at the keypad. It startled her when she realized that she was typing:

"At the base of the Deeds Carillon is a quotation from Henry Wadsworth Longfellow..."

29

The file in front of Bill Slater was two inches thick, and he was contemplating his strategy for addressing the grand jury. In his mind's eye he could look around the table and identify the people who would see his point of view and those who would be vocally opposed to the prospect of handing down an indictment that named Barker Fornesby. He knew his evidence was slim, and convincing the sixteen jurors would not be an easy task. What he needed was a way to make the grand jury aware of the newspaper interviews with Deb Walker and Barker Fornesby. Elizabeth Carnaby had done a masterful job of framing the nurse's comments about family frustrations against a backdrop of euthanasia. The following day's article that quoted Fornesby was less useful. It appeared very sympathetic with no references to mercy killing. Still, it was printed under the series heading 'Euthanasia: Mercy or Murder?' and the minds of the jurors could be pointed in that direction.

Physically and mentally, Slater felt fit and alert. His senses were honed, and he was pleased that he was, at last, to be able to expose the hidden crime of Barker Fornesby, a man who had a gift for hiding behind a facade of decency. He looked at his watch. Sometime in the next hour, he would be called to present his evidence and instructions to the grand jury. He read his presentation outline over again, but it was already well established in his mind.

30

The Dayton Daily Herald was spread out on the McGowan's kitchen table. Davis had been told of the Euthanasia series by several church members who thought it could become the basis of an ethics class. The articles were thought-provoking, but today's article was particularly captivating. It was an interview with Barker Fornesby, and Davis was puzzled at its inclusion. He sensed that something was terribly wrong. Remembering that he had Barker's office phone number, he retrieved his appointment calendar and called the number. A woman's voice answered.

"Mr. Fornesby's office, this is Margaret speaking."

"Yes," said Davis, "is Barker there?"

"I'm sorry," answered Margaret, "Mr. Fornesby is on a six month leave of absence."

Puzzled at the message, Davis blurted out, "Margaret, this is Davis McGowan, Barker's minister. How can I get hold of him?"

"Oh, Dr. McGowan," said Margaret remembering the time that the two had met when the minister had come for a lunchtime appointment with her boss. "Actually, Barker is here, but we've been getting so many calls since the article came out this morning. I'm sure he'd want to talk with you. I'll ask."

"Margaret," came Davis' reply. "Is it true about the six month leave of absence?"

"As far as I know," she answered. "It caught me off guard, too. Evidently there must have been a high-powered meeting in the middle of the night or early this morning."

"Whose idea was it that he take the leave?" inquired Davis.

"I don't know," replied the secretary. "Maybe he'll tell you. Rumor has it that he wanted to resign outright, but the president convinced him to just take a leave."

"Why?"

"Like I said, maybe he'll talk to you. Let me get him." There was a long silence, then a man's voice.

"Yes, Davis. I'm glad you called." It was Barker's voice.

"What's going on Barker? I called to talk about the article in the paper, and Margaret says you're taking a leave of absence?"

"Well, I know it's confusing and I'm probably just as confused as anyone," came Barker's answer. "I really can't tell you any more than I'm taking some time off. Matt and I could use the time together, and well, some things might come out in the next few days that could embarrass the company."

"What in the world are you talking about?" responded Davis.

"Okay," said Barker, "I'll level with you, but please-- this is privileged information, right?"

"Alright, I won't tell anyone, not even Beth."

"They are still trying to figure out how Angie got so much insulin in her system, and it's being turned over to a grand jury to see if an indictment is in order." Barker's words hit Davis without warning.

"You're not saying that this is going to go to trial?"

"If an indictment is handed down, they'll try to take it to trial, but I will never let them do that," said Fornesby with a conviction in his voice that Davis did not doubt, though he did not understand the comment. How could he stop a trial?

"But what can you do?" responded Davis after the shock had subsided.

"Never mind," was the quick reply. "What I want is for you to stay with Matt if anything happens. Okay? Promise?"

"Sure," said Davis, "but..." He was cut off.

"Just help him keep a perspective. You'll know what I mean. I can't talk any more. Thanks for everything, friend." The receiver went dead in Davis' hand. Slowly, he replaced it in the cradle and sat down, deep in thought.

31

"Ladies and Gentlemen, I'll be quite honest with you," began Bill Slater, "we don't have a clear-cut case here, but a crime may have been committed and then covered up. Some of you may call some of the evidence 'circumstantial', but I will argue that there has been only one person who has consistently tried to block this investigation, and that person is likely to be a murderer. As I present the scenario of what happened, some of you will be tempted to think that we may be dealing with a crime of compassion, a mercy killing, if you will. Again, I contend that there is reason to believe that there are extenuating circumstances that would call this conclusion into question. Nevertheless, I believe that you will find that we are dealing with a case of murder, either in the first degree or voluntary manslaughter."

Slater allowed the weight of his words to sink in before continuing. "The case is that of Angela Fornesby," he looked quickly around the room to see if the name seemed to invoke any recognition. A few jurors seemed to raise their eyebrows and he hoped that it meant that the morning paper had planted the name 'Fornesby' in their minds.

"Mrs. Fornesby was a diabetic who was recently diagnosed as having cancer. I know that some will immediately think that this woman was dying, as if that would be a reason to not look any farther, but, we have the testimony of her physician that her diabetes was under control and she was in the early stages of chemotherapy with every prospect of sending the cancer into remission.

In other words, she could have had a fairly normal life for years.

"Now, the night she was released from the hospital, she died at home. The coroner has determined that the cause of death, put simply, was an overdose of insulin. Again, some would say that this could have been accidental, but I remind you that Mrs. Fornesby was a diabetic for most of her adult life and no one in her family was new or untrained in the procedure for testing or administering her medication.

"In fact, the family kept a log of every injection and every glucose reading. That log was not surrendered voluntarily to the police, but a detective had to retrieve it in person after several requests. A study of the log indicates that every injection was appropriate, and it in no way helps us determine how the lethal dose entered Mrs. Fornesby's body.

"In front of you are various transcripts. The medical notes and charts are there, as well as notes of a phone conversation that I had with Dr. Carew. The family minister's testimony to the coroner is also there. He says that Mrs. Fornesby's attitude prior to release from the hospital was hopeful and positive.

"You see, it is a mystery. We have a woman who wanted to live, with a diagnosis that would suggest that she would have years left to her, and she dies of an overdose of her own medication. We also have uncovered," Slater hesitated, but it was his only real physical evidence... "we have also uncovered an insulin syringe. It was found under the mattress, as though hastily hidden. It contained traces of insulin. It is the only used syringe found in the house. The visiting nurse had taken all the others for disposal when she left the evening Angela Fornesby died. It could quite possibly be the murder weapon. The insulin was drawn after all the other needles had been taken away.

"The next question is of motive and opportunity. Of course, anyone who Mrs. Fornesby trusted to give her injections would have opportunity. Motive is something less obvious. During the police investigation, however, we learned of another curious connection. Several days after Mrs. Fornesby's death, her husband was seen in the company of another woman. On further investigation, we have discovered that they had seen each other regularly during his wife's hospitalization. In fact, the woman in question is a nurse who would have complete knowledge of Mrs. Fornesby's condition.

"In summary, what do we have? An unexplained dose of insulin, a husband who has been administering injections, and a nurse girlfriend named Deb Walker who is waiting in the wings." Slater noticed the same eyebrows being raised at the mention of Deb's name. "Good," he thought to himself, "some of these people have retained what they read in the paper!"

"With that, I leave this is your capable hands. Copies of the testimony are in the files in front of you, and I'll leave my file here as well. Thank you for your time." He was quite proud of his summary, and could tell already that this case would not be considered lightly.

32

The grand jury deliberations were going nowhere after three hours of debate. Most of the jurors had long ago lost their ability to concentrate as the more vocal members went around and around in circular arguments. The people seemed divided into three camps, those who felt that a love triangle was a powerful motive for murder, those who thought the evidence of the triangle's existence was virtually non-existent, and those who were totally confused. The one thing that sustained the debate was the fact that all agreed that there was an unexplained death open for their consideration.

"And you think that 'Mr. Fancy Suit' is above having a sweetie on the side," bullied Kenny Lewis, a union steward at the local auto assembly plant.

"I don't know," pleaded Corrine Saunders who had dug in her heels against Lewis' hard-nosed attitude. "It could be that they are just friends."

"Right! And the tooth fairy reads dental x-rays," continued Kenny Lewis.

"Does anyone else want to speak?" pleaded Adam Nelson, the beleaguered foreman. He was beyond his skill to keep the conversation moving ahead, and hoping that someone in the group could reestablish some sense of order. Finally, a quiet member of the jury spoke out. It was Jasmine Sullivan, a welfare mother who was attending the local community college.

"I think we need to talk to the minister again," she offered. All eyes turned to her. She had spent a great deal of time reading transcripts and had opted out of the verbal challenges.

"What do you mean?" asked the foreman.

"Well, we keep talking about whether this Mr. Fornesby fellow had a reason to do it, and we can't decide. What if we found out that Mrs. Fornesby had thought about ending her own life?" The simple reasoning seemed to provide another way to look at the problem. Adam Nelson, the foreman, jumped on it.

"Can you say more about what you mean?" encouraged Adam.

"Well, we can't be positive that Mr. Fornesby did anything without some more proof. But if Mrs. Fornesby had thought about killing herself, wouldn't that make us always wonder..."

"Yes," said Corrine, "there'd always be what Mr. Slater called 'reasonable doubt'."

"But the minister didn't know anything," protested Kenny Lewis.

"He wasn't asked," persisted Jasmine. "That's why I kept reading over and over again this paper that tells what he said before. He was asked about what happened that night, the night Mrs. Fornesby died, but he didn't say nothing about when he talked to her before, when she was in the hospital. I figured that might be something I'd tell my Reverend."

In the end, not everyone was happy, but everyone agreed that a second subpoena would be issued to require further testimony from Dr. Davis McGowan.

33

Beth and Davis McGowan met following work at a restaurant for dinner and a drink. They took their time, for this was to be one of their rare evenings together. On most week nights, Davis would have a meeting at the church with some volunteer committee. When they returned home at about 7:30, however, the red light on the answering machine was flashing.

"Let's hope that it's for one of the kids," said Davis, pushing the message retrieval button. The machine beeped, rewound itself, and began to play back. It was a woman's voice, a voice that Davis did not recognize.

"Reverend McGowan," the voice stated, "you don't know me. My name is Deb Walker and I'm a friend of Barker Fornesby. We need to talk as soon as possible." The message ended with her giving a phone number and was followed by a series of sharp tones before the self-winding mechanism returned the tape to its reset position.

"What do you suppose that's about?" said Davis to Beth, "and do I dare let it go until tomorrow?"

"I don't think you can. You were pretty tight-lipped when you mentioned that you phoned Barker this afternoon, but I can read you well enough to know that you thought something was going on."

"Am I that transparent?" asked Davis. Of course he knew that Beth was right, and this was a message that he could not ignore. He listened to the recording one more time to make sure of the phone number and made the phone call. As he was speaking, the doorbell rang and Beth went to answer it. She returned about the time Davis hung up. Their faces were mirror images of each other's in terms of showing confused concern.

"That was a sheriff's deputy with this," said Beth, handing him a subpoena for an appearance before the grand jury at 10:00 the following morning.

"And I'm supposed to meet this Deb Walker at my office in twenty minutes," added Davis.

"What about?" queried Beth.

"I'm not sure," confided Davis. "She wants to give me something or show me something. She sounds very concerned that Barker is going to do something crazy, and I guess I wouldn't believe her if he hadn't been so weird this morning on the phone."

"And what do you know that a grand jury wouldn't already know from your previous testimony?" puzzled Beth.

"Beats me," was Davis' reply. "I hope I don't learn something tonight that I will wish I didn't know when they question me tomorrow. Sorry for the short evening, but maybe this won't take too long?"

"I'll leave the light on," said Beth, kissing him on the cheek. She had grown used to the fact that other people seemed to own her husband's time, but she knew that he didn't like it any more than she did.

34

Davis felt a little on the spot as he took his seat at the end of the large walnut conference table. Around the table sat the members of the grand jury and one face that looked familiar. It was the man who had been at the coroner's interview, the man from the prosecutor's office that had referred to him as a 'hostile witness'. Bill Slater made eye contact with Davis, then quickly turned away.

"Reverend McGowan, you may be wondering why we called you in here," began Adam Nelson, the jury foreman, "but we have some questions about Angela Fornesby that some of us think you may be able to answer."

"I'll try," answered Davis, trying to sound calm and cooperative.

"We have read the testimony that you gave to the coroner about the night you were called out to the Fornesby's. Can you tell us about Mr. Fornesby's state of mind on that night?"

Davis paused for a moment. "He was very quiet. I suppose he was in shock. I guess that is what I expect when I go into such situations. People turn in on themselves pretty much, but with Barker it was quite a contrast."

"What do you mean?" encouraged Adam.

"It's just that Barker Fornesby is never at a loss for words or action, but that night he was just drained. Like I said, in shock."

"When you were cleaning up, after the deputy left, did you see this chart?" The foreman slid the insulin log to Davis who took it and gave it a studied look.

"Yes, I believe so, or something quite like it," responded Davis.

"Do you know what it is?" continued the questioner.

"Yes, it's the record of Angie's, Mrs. Fornesby's, insulin doses. She had been a diabetic for many years," he added.

The foreman continued. "When the coroner questioned you before, you were asked if Barker ever talked to you about euthanasia. You didn't give a very clear answer, and in light of recent developments, we were wondering if you could comment on it further?"

"You mean the articles in the newspaper?" Davis said. Bill Slater sat up straight. "No, I never spoke with Barker about mercy killing, and I can't tell you why he was interviewed in relation to that subject by the Herald." Slater was not pleased with McGowan's response.

"We are aware of the newspaper articles, but they are not really a part of the evidence that we are investigating," said Nelson. "But did you ever discuss euthanasia with anyone in connection with the Fornesby's?"

Davis took a long thoughtful pause. "Actually, I did on several occasions. Well, it really wasn't exactly about mercy killing. Angela and I once talked about her 'living will'. She had said that she and Barker both had signed one."

"But a 'living will' has nothing to do with mercy killing." All heads turned to see Bill Slater break his silence with the statement.

"I know," replied Davis, "but after we talked about not wanting to be resuscitated, Angie asked what I thought about suicide.

"If I remember, I made some fairly theoretical comments. I think I said something to the effect that it depends on whether you're trying to choose death as a way to run away from your problems, or because you recognize that your life is really over, and that all that lies ahead is destructive to yourself and the family. As I said, I don't exactly remember, except that the tone was pretty unemotional, and I didn't feel that she was speaking out of any depression or lack of hope."

"Do you remember what she said?" asked a juror.

"I don't know where I stand on this kind of testimony," said McGowan nervously. "I don't know how much of what I'm saying should really be considered privileged information between a church member and a pastor, but I can't see how it would hurt anything since Angela is dead. The truth is that she talked about everything like it was a discussion in an ethics class, and then she said something I'll never forget. During the discussion, we had both been fairly detached, but at the end she said, 'It's something that I know I'd have to consider if I felt that I was looking at the prospect of what a long death would do to my family.' I guess it was the way she said it that was different. It was a personal conviction."

Davis' testimony caused a stir in the room, but the real reaction came from Bill Slater who rose to his feet and walked out of the chamber.

"Do you think that Angela Fornesby committed suicide?" asked the Foreman.

"I suppose she could have," said McGowan, "but I doubt it."

"Then how would you explain the overdose of insulin?" came the final question.

"Now you are asking for an opinion, not facts, but I'll tell you what I believe. I know the whole family, and I can say that I believe that the whole thing was an accident. Her insulin tolerance changed or something, but I don't believe it was suicide or mercy killing."

35

The British judicial system gives juries a third option to deliver in place of the verdicts 'guilty' or 'not-guilty'. Charges can be 'not-proven', which is a sort of technical middle ground for juries who believe that the defendant is guilty, but that compelling evidence had not been presented. That option might have provided this grand jury with more room for their debate. While they were not deciding on guilt or innocence, they had to decide whether enough evidence existed to make the pursuit of justice more than a wild goose chase. The facts were clear. A woman was dead. It was evidence that was missing, and in lieu of proof, personal opinion became the focus of debate.

"I think that Fornesby just got away with murder," pleaded Kenny Lewis who was still convinced that an indictment was in order, but his support was fading fast.

"Unless someone steps forward to confess, there's no way to prove anything as long as that minister will say that the lady had talked about suicide," added a heretofore quiet juror.

All in all, it took the grand jury less than thirty minutes to come to the conclusion that no indictments could be handed down. In the end, it had become quite clear that without further substantial evidence, no prosecution would be successful because there would always be a reasonable doubt hovering over the case with regard to the possibility that Angela might have taken her own life.

Within the jury itself, opinion remained divided, but Bill Slater was livid. After four drinks at the Courthouse Lounge, he convinced himself that he had earned the right to anonymously tell Barker Fornesby where to go. A pay phone in the entryway proved to be the weapon of choice. He dialed the Fornesby home, and Barker answered.

"Fornesby?" Slater said curtly. "I want you to know that you sure got your money's worth out of your church membership. Next time the plate goes 'round slip in a little something for McGowan. The lyin' creep sure pulled your bacon out of the fire. If your wife committed suicide, I'm Father Christmas." With a smirk, he hung up the phone, and a very distressed Barker Fornesby did the same.

36

Davis McGowan was sitting in his office when an exhausted Barker Fornesby walked through his open door.

"Can we talk?" Barker asked.

"Sure, have a seat," said Davis, moving from behind his desk to close the door and take a seat opposite Fornesby.

134

"I don't understand what happened. Maybe I don't understand anything?" began Barker. "I take it that you testified that you thought Angie committed suicide?"

"Not exactly, Barker. I testified that Angie and I had once openly discussed the idea of suicide, and that she was not totally opposed to it. What I said was that I thought it was an accident."

"Did Angie really think about suicide?" questioned Barker. "We never talked about such a thing."

"Neither did we, Barker. I lied." A look of disbelief came over Fornesby's face. Davis continued, "You see, I not only think it was an accident, I know it was an accident. I know that it was Matt who gave Angie the lethal dose."

Barker began to protest, then hesitated, put his face in his hands and began to sob, as the pent up emotions flowed from his shaking body. The two sat together for some time before Fornesby could express himself again. "How did you find out?"

"I'd like to think that I could have figured it out myself," began McGowan. "Maybe I would have when they showed me the insulin log at the grand jury. I remembered that Matt once told me that he had given his mother insulin on the night she died, but every entry on that log was in your handwriting. I could have figured out that the last dose wasn't recorded and that was the extra insulin, the overdose that led to Angie's death. But that wasn't the real log, was it?"

"No, but how did you know that?" asked Barker.

"I knew it because you have a friend who cares about you," answered Davis who went to his desk drawer and retrieved a piece of paper. He handed it to Barker who recognized it immediately as the original insulin log.

"I gave that to Deb," said Fornesby, almost to himself.

"And she gave it to me last night," offered McGowan. "I know she promised to keep your secret and keep the log away from everyone, but she knew what you were planning. She told me that you were going to plead guilty to any indictment that was handed down in order to keep this thing out of the courtroom. When she said that, I understood what you meant the other day when you said that you wouldn't let this go to trial."

"I had to keep it out of a public forum," offered Barker. "It was because Matt would be in the courtroom, or even be called to testify. They'd start to add up the insulin doses, and he would wonder why the injection he gave was not on the log when he very plainly wrote it there.

"It really was an accident," continued Barker. "I had just gone downstairs with the nurse so that we could talk privately. She had just started an IV drip with the insulin in the IV solution. Angie was with me when the nurse explained it, but somehow it must not have registered. Matt and Angie didn't realize that there was a change in the way the medication was being administered, and they went ahead with the procedure that we had been following. It was a terrible mistake."

"When did you realize that, Barker?" asked Davis.

"When I discovered Angie's body. The log was sitting there with the sharpie right next to it. It just jumped out at me. I realized what had happened and I didn't want Matt to know that he had accidentally killed his mother. Can you imagine what that would do to him? You know how much he loved her!"

Davis nodded.

"Anyway," continued Fornesby, "I hid the log and the syringe, and then called you. Nobody asked too much, nobody questioned Matt at all, and I thought that maybe the report would come back without a lot of questions because Angie was very sick. But then they kept asking for the log, and I stalled as long as I could."

"That's when you made up the fake report," added McGowan.

"It's not really fake," corrected Fornesby. "It was just that no one ever asked Matt anything. Originally, I thought of writing a new report and altering the times that the injections were given, but I knew that if it was subjected to any kind of scrutiny, someone might see that I'd forged Matt's entry. So I just copied the log by hand and left off that last dose. Since it was all my handwriting, I figured no one would know."

"Unless Matt saw it, right?" said Davis.

"That's right, unless Matt saw it. But no one ever asked him anything. Does the world always ignore kids? Anyway, when they added up all the doses from my report and the visiting nurse's report everything checked out."

"Except that, somehow, Angie had gotten an unreported overdose," continued Davis. "So that's when you decided that you'd confess to euthanasia if necessary."

"You've been with Matt. How do you think that he would handle it if he found out that he injected the lethal dose? I figured he'd forgive me in time if I could convince him that I did it and that Angie wanted me to."

"In other words, you'd take the hit. You'd allow him to hate you, at least in the short term, rather than bear the weight of what really happened," concluded Davis.

"That's about it. Am I an awful person?" asked Barker.

"I'm the one who committed perjury so that you could maintain your story," answered Davis. "What does that make me? Once I understood what happened I realized that I was in a position to help you keep the truth from Matt, and, like you, I'm not sure what he would do if he knew the truth. Matt gave his mother insulin because he loved her, but the dose she needed was already slowly dripping into her bloodstream in the IV solution."

"If he was ever to find that out, he'd never forgive himself," said Fornesby, "and I would have lost both Matt and Angie in one death."

A long silence came over the room as Fornesby sunk deeply into his own thoughts. Davis broke the silence, "what about the syringe that they found under the mattress? Is that the one that killed Angie?"

"No," retorted Barker. "I could not abide that one. I knew that it was evidence. It probably had Matt's fingerprints on it, so I got rid of it."

"Then what did they find in the room?"

"That was an afterthought. I wanted to get rid of the needle, so I gave it to Deb at the same time I gave her the log. I knew she could drop it off at the hospital and it would be gone forever with all the tons of medical waste that they trash every day. But then, when they kept pushing me for the log, I realized that they were not going to drop the witch hunt. If there was no needle in the room, the suspicious minds would have a field day. They'd figure that a murderer carried it off. So I filled a syringe with insulin and shot it down the drain."

"And stuffed it under the mattress," added Davis.

"Yes, that's right," confirmed Fornesby. "I figured that it would create more questions than it would solve, and would at least remove the argument that someone took it. And more than that, I knew that Matt hadn't touched it."

"Even Angie could have slid it under there after injecting herself," added Davis. "That would suggest the possibility that it was a suicide."

"I hadn't thought of that," considered Barker, "but I guess you're right. God, I hate all this! The truth might kill my son, and all I wanted to do was crawl in the grave with Angie!"

There was nothing to say in response to Barker's final comment. The two sat in silence for an eternity, neither looking at the other. Barker stood up and walked toward the window. He retrieved a handkerchief from his back pocket and wiped his eyes.

"You know what struck me that morning? After you left the house?" asked Barker.

"No," replied Davis.

"I walked out to the car with you. I don't remember that we said anything, it was just quiet. You drove off and I stood there. The air was brisk and the sky was beginning to glow. It was absolutely beautiful. And I didn't want it to be beautiful."

*   *   *

When time flowed back into sequence, Davis asked the question that had been bothering him. "Couldn't you have told the prosecutor and kept it all very secret?"

"I didn't feel that I could take that chance with Matt's life. Maybe I've just been in business too long. People always make promises they can't keep, and in the end, remaining quiet would have been better. It's like when a company develops a new process for something like a copy machine. They submit the specs to the patent office, but they know that if the information becomes public, their competitors will be imitating them before the patent is granted. The trick is to provide enough data to get the patent without actually revealing the process. If you ever tried to build a machine from actual patent specifications, you might be surprised to find that the innovation won't work. Secrecy is a safer form of security than the patent laws. That was my hope, but now you know. The circle is growing."

"Who all knows?" questioned McGowan.

"There are now four of us. You, me, Ted Clarke, my security chief who kept me informed about the investigation, and Deb Walker," confessed Barker.

"Deb won't tell, don't worry about her," added Davis. "She was in a state when she told me, and she only did so because she was as fearful for you as you were for Matt. She seems like a very good person."

"She was the friend that I needed when Angie was sick, and especially after the night she died," offered Fornesby. "She was someone outside my circle of friends that I could trust. I gave her the insulin log figuring that the prosecutor's office would never know that I even knew her, but somehow they discovered our friendship and wanted to make it into something it wasn't. I still don't know how they found out. See what I mean about the need for secrecy?"

"I think your secret is safe among the four of us, and Matt will never know what he did, or how very much his father loves him."

"I hope he never learns the truth, but as to knowing how much I love him, that's something that I've resolved to show him. I've been away too long, emotionally, that is, and I see that now. It may be the one good thing that I've learned in all this."

"Barker, what are you going to do?"

"Well, the president wouldn't let me resign, so I can get my job back, but I'm not going to be in too much of a hurry. Financially, we'll be okay for a while, and if I spend down some of the savings, that'll be better than what I've been doing," said Barker.

"And what's that?" queried McGowan.

"I've been spending down my time for the wrong reasons. There's a young man living with me that I hardly know, and I need to waste some time with him."

37

The sun was shining and the air was less humid than usual when Davis decided to make a call at the Fornesby's house. It had been a week since Davis had spoken with Barker in his office, and he was beginning to hope that no news was good news. When he pulled into the drive, he noticed that the front door was propped open. As he approached the house on foot, he called out. "Anyone at home?"

"We're in here, Davis," came Barker's voice from within.

Entering the house, McGowan found himself in a maze of drop cloths and surrounded by the distinctive smell of latex paint.

"You're just in time to grab a roller and help," said Barker as he stepped around the corner between the kitchen and the dining room. "Matt and I are catching up on some fix-up chores. Want to help?"

"I'm on to your tricks, Barker," he said, "besides, I've read this one in *The Adventures of Tom Sawyer.*"

"Oh well, I tried. Right, Matt?" The young man stuck his head around the corner, and then moved to stand next to his father. Davis was pleased to see him smiling again. "We've just now started to paint the dining room wall. Want to see?"

"Sure," said Davis, catching the positive mood that was being expressed. Not much of the wall had been painted yet, but one spot was carefully rolled out. Davis recognized it as the place where Matt had repaired a dent in the wall. "It looks good," offered Davis, "in fact, it looks very good! When you're done, do you want to come over to my house?"

"No thanks," bantered Barker, "we don't want to lose our amateur status. And you're right, it does look very good." He put an arm around his son.

"Well," responded Davis, "I don't want to stop progress or interfere with drying paint. In fact, I came over here to see if I could dodge my own work by hiding out with you guys, and you two are absolutely no help at all," concluded McGowan. He waved an arm and started for the door.

"Davis," called Barker behind him. McGowan stopped and turned back. "Davis, I thought you'd like to know that Matt thinks I should go back to work." He turned and threw a wink to Matt.

"And what do you think?" asked Davis.

"I made a deal with him," said Fornesby. "I told him that I'd go back as soon as we've found a trilobite. Now I ask you, does that seem fair?"

"It seems more than fair, Barker, but what does Matt think?" Matt's smile was the only answer.

"Yes," repeated Davis, "It's a fair deal, one of the best I've heard in a long time."

143

38

As Davis drove off, old feelings began to well up within him. Within a quarter of a mile, he pulled off the road and into a neighborhood park. In the distance a shrill whistle sounded as two teams of diminutive soccer players squared off against each other. He found a parking space well away from the activity and rolled down the window. Already the air was hinting that autumn would come swiftly. The dry summer was already casting its spell on the foliage, and above a grass-covered field, a small bird of prey hovered.

It had been good to see Matt and Barker working side by side. Angie's death would not be an easy thing to overcome, but for now at least, the two seemed willing to face it together. Barker's secret would be safe among the co-conspirators. No one else would ever need know of the second insulin log. Davis wondered if Barker realized that he, too, held a secret. Davis had lied under oath, but it was a sin that he could live with. Others might not be so understanding.

The hawk continued to wing overhead in ever-widening circles. It seemed all alone in a huge sky, and yet it flew with a purpose known only to itself. Davis watched. The words of one of his own poems came to his mind. He had written it during a flight to an out-of-town meeting:

> Imprisoned in the cell,
> I see the clouds,
>   but feel no wind,

no breath to wash me clean.
Falcon is not envious of fume or power,
  but I of her,
For she wings free,
  soaring with silent strokes
    in an ocean of air.

What does she see?
  Is it hare or mouse or shadow of light?
Can she see beyond the light,
  and glimpse her own circle of self?

Falcon is no dreamer,
  she just glides freely,
    and in that,
  is more wise than I,
with fewer fears and no remorse.

But does she love?
  And if love bears the price of other emotions,
I will love,
  I will fly free,
    I will soar as Falcon in an ocean of air.

Davis turned the key and the car sprang to life. He
had five minutes to get to the home of a young couple.
Their premature baby had died in the neonatal unit
yesterday of an uncontrollable brain-bleed. Davis had sat
with them in the room as they held the small body. Now
he was going to their home to talk about a service to

recognize their loss. If he would have allowed himself to name his own feelings at that moment, he would have known that his old enemy was back. He did not give it much thought as he drove off. He was alone.

Billy Kirschbaum

Covenant Church is situated in a residential area of Dayton and is adjacent to the on-ramp linking South Main Street to the outer-belt which skirts the metropolitan area. At peak hours the traffic pattern in the intersection mimics bumper cars, and the church staff grew to expect strangers seeking a phone in order to report an accident. The emergence of cell phone technology had reduced this particular pilgrimage significantly. It did not, however, do anything to deter the flow of transients to the front door.

Many people cling to the romantic notion that church doors should always be open to the needy or to some "fugitive soul" seeking sanctuary. The reality is that church buildings are subject to vandalism and staff members are seen as an easy mark by those with violent intentions. In the case of Covenant Church, the line between an open door and a safe work environment contained a security camera, an intercom, and a remote door release.

When the secretary, Connie Foster, was alone in the building, her instructions were to err on the side of caution. When the full staff was present, caution was mostly thrown to the wind. Within the staff, there was a running joke that the personnel committee had inserted

147

the phrase "and other duties as assigned" in the senior pastor's position description to cover Davis McGowan's responsibility as church bouncer and security guard.

When Billy Kirschbaum suddenly appeared in the church office, Connie picked up the phone and paged Davis. Her voice quivered as she spoke. The vagrant had entered so silently that he seemed an uncalled apparition.

"Do we have any Mickey D coupons?" she asked. It was a coded message that McGowan understood. "Mickey D" meant that someone was in the outer office, and Connie was being pushed outside her comfort zone.

"Hi, can I help you?" said Davis emerging from his private office. His manner was calm and polite, and his greeting dissolved all the tension in the room.

"Are you the Pastor?" asked the stranger.

"Yes, I'm Davis McGowan. What can I do for you?"

"My name is Billy Kirschbaum," said the man. "I'm trying to make my way to New Hampshire, and I really would like to get a cup of coffee and something to eat."

"Well, coffee is not a problem around here," said Davis. Connie was already moving back toward the alcove where the coffeemaker lived. "And, I'm sure we can get you a meal, as well. How do you like your coffee?"

"Black." Connie raised her head and nodded in recognition.

Kirschbaum lowered his backpack to the floor. Attached to the bag was a canvas pouch in the recognizable shape of a guitar. He was a small man with dark hair and a few days' growth of stubble. He didn't know it, but he had already made a positive impression on McGowan. It was nothing in his unassuming character that led to this reaction; it was his unabashed honesty.

It is easy for a minister to become cynical of people who come looking for a handout. The cynicism comes, not from the reality of human need, but the games that are so often played by the not-so-needy. Scammers usually begin by saying that they need to talk to the pastor alone. Once in private, they deliver their well-worn speeches. After decades in the ministry, McGowan had heard it all, from families swept away by the Great Johnstown Flood to people who really crave a new Bible (and maybe twenty bucks).

Davis' policy was not to argue, but also not to give out cash. Admittedly, there were times when he wanted to say: "You are much too young to have lost a wife in Johnstown in 1889," but there were other floods in that region and he was not willing to argue the finer points of history. Instead of cash, Covenant Church had developed a policy of helping people with the basics. If they needed gasoline, they had an arrangement with a nearby filling station. For groceries there was a food pantry, and for transients, the code words *Mickey D coupons* took on a more ordinary meaning.

Billy Kirschbaum did not ask for a private audience, nor did he have a long story. He was simply hungry. When Connie handed the Styrofoam cup to Billy, Davis moved to the file cabinet where the fast food coupons

149

were kept. He grabbed four books from the stash and went back to where Kirschbaum had camped out.

"We don't usually give this many coupons to an individual," he said, "but it sounds like you're going to be on the road for awhile. There's a restaurant just two blocks north of here, but they should also be usable wherever you go."

"Thank you," said Billy. He tucked the coupon books under a flap in his pack and lifted it to one shoulder. Davis stepped forward walking with him to the door. "Reverend, can I ask a big favor?" added Kirschbaum.

"Go ahead."

"Can you drive me an exit or two down the highway? Every time I try to hitch a ride, the police pick me up. It's happened three times, and I just want to get out of this town."

Davis understood the request. In this community the police cars were Volvos and it was understood that people who looked like they didn't belong were treated that way as well. "Okay," he said, "I can take you to the next exit. It's beyond the city limits and there are a bunch of fast food places where you can get something to eat."

A wave of relief came over Billy's face, but Connie Foster looked on the edge of panic.

Davis turned to the secretary and said, "I'll be back in a half an hour." Kirschbaum and McGowan left the building and headed toward the parking lot. Billy's duffle and guitar were thrown into the back seat, and the two climbed into the front of the small economy car. Within a few minutes of the engine firing, they were accelerating down the entrance ramp and onto the freeway.

"Sounds like you've got a long journey ahead," began McGowan. Billy paused before speaking. Davis wondered if he was collecting his thoughts or deciding whether this was a time to tell his story.

"My name is Kirschbaum," he began, "that's German for *cherry tree*. The way I figure it is that I was given that name because I had to do some growing before I could bear fruit. I grew up in New Hampshire. I had parents and a family there, but I really screwed things up, maybe, fifteen years ago. I got into drugs and hit the road. About a year ago, I sobered up. I started singing for people. I'd go any place where they'd listen. I started on the streets, but ended up playing mostly at nursing homes. I met this minister; he'd take me around with him to play when he went there to visit. I'd always start out, 'I'm Billy Kirschbaum and that means cherry tree!' The old people really liked my singing, so I kept going. All the while, this Reverend and I would talk. One day he asks, 'Billy, is there something you need to do?' And, I knew there was." Kirschbaum stopped for a moment and looked out the side window toward the housing sub-divisions that were blurring past. Davis let him live in the silence, and he began again.

"The way I figure it is that it's easy to pretend that everything is all right, and as long as the pretending works, things never will be right." Davis turned in amazement at the homeless man's words. Billy never broke his gaze from the road ahead. Somehow

151

McGowan knew that Kirschbaum wasn't really seeing anything through the windshield.

"The old people were like my folks, the ones I left when I walked out all those years ago. When I walked out on them, I didn't leave them with much except my hate and anger. I've got to try and fix that so I can stop pretending and have a real life." He turned toward Davis and their eyes met. Davis nodded his understanding.

"I'm heading for home, and I'm not going to pretend to fix my life without actually trying. My family is important to me. I know it now, but I've never told them that."

By this time, McGowan was pulling into a parking space. Billy and he got out of the car. He opened the rear door and Billy stepped up to retrieve his belongings. He slung the pack over one shoulder and turned to Davis.

"Thank you," he said.

"Good luck, Billy Cherry Tree," said McGowan, shaking the hand that Billy had extended to him.

Davis did not remember the drive back to the church. Fortunately the car was on autopilot, and he only became aware of where he was when he turned off the ignition key. As he walked toward the office entrance, he saw Connie, the church secretary, and Linda, the associate pastor, anxiously watching from behind the glass doors of the vestibule. As he approached, they moved back into the office.

"I was about ready to call the police," said Connie, as he entered.

Linda added her concern, "When I was told that you got into your car with a transient, I thought you must be crazy. What were you thinking, Davis?"

"I must have been the only one who wasn't worried. Billy's okay; you could tell that from the start."

"Still, Davis, you're not that tough! He could have had a gun!" Linda didn't let up. It was obvious that he had traumatized the staff.

"I suppose," he answered. "Didn't seem like much of a risk at the time." Davis busied himself by looking into the inbox to see if there was anything new. "Were there any calls while I was gone?"

The question was a call to normalcy, or maybe a declaration that the current conversation was over.

"You want to know what's really odd?" queried Davis. The two women turned back to him. "I have just spent thirty minutes talking to a homeless vagrant who might even have some mental issues, but I agree with everything he said."

Freeze Tag

"Davis!" Connie Foster's voice sounded over the telephone paging system, "Richard Watkins is on line one."

McGowan lifted the handset. "Thanks, Connie," he said before pressing the flashing button to retrieve the parked call. "This is Davis."

Rick Watkins' voice took off with his typical animated cadence. "Did you talk with Bill Slater?"

The mention of the name halted McGowan and drove him back four years to when he had first come in contact with a Bill Slater. He had been drawn into a grand jury inquiry into the death of a parishioner named Angela Fornesby. She had died of an overdose of insulin, and her husband was considered a possible suspect. Davis was their minister at the time, and his testimony about Angie's state of mind had made the jury drop its investigation. For some reason, the prosecutor considered McGowan's statement an out-and-out lie. Bill Slater was that prosecutor.

"I don't understand," said McGowan.

"Bill Slater," repeated Watkins, "he was in church yesterday, didn't you see him?"

"No, but I'll see if he signed in as a visitor."

"Do you know who he is?" Watkins didn't wait for a reply, "He's going to be a hot contender for the mayor's race. It would be a real coup if we could get him to join."

"Well, we usually send a team to call on all the first time visitors, so I'll make sure that we match him up with callers who can speak on his social level."

"This calls for more than that, Davis. Bill Slater should command the attention of the senior minister. It would be good if you made that call yourself. Do you understand what I'm saying?"

"Yes, Rick, I get it, and I'll make sure that Slater gets a good introduction to the congregation. Have you heard from Carolyn?" Davis was aware that Rick's wife had lost a sister in Wyoming and was away helping her niece and nephew to clear out her house. While he was concerned about a parishioner, he was also happy to divert the conversation.

"I haven't talked to her since last Friday," said Watkins. "She expects to be home by the end of the week."

"Well, tell her that we're thinking about her," said Davis, "and I'll talk to her next week. Thanks for calling my attention to Slater's visit."

"Then you'll take care of it?"

"Sure," said McGowan. When he hung up the phone, he knew what he would do. Bill Slater would be greeted like any other visitor. In a moment he would go out to the main office where Connie Foster would be sorting through the names of first time visitors who had

155

attended church the day before. For the moment, however, he wanted to recall his first encounter with Slater. Why would he show up in church? Clearly, Slater had no respect for him. He remembered Barker Fornesby's chagrin when a clearly intoxicated Bill Slater called him to say that his minister had lied through his teeth to the grand jury.

When Barker's son graduated from high school, he was free to accept a new position in Chicago. Matt was attending Northwestern University, and the two were still exploring the new realities of their family without Angie. Davis rose from his chair and went out to the main office.

"Connie, did you see where we have a visitor named 'Bill Slater' in church yesterday?"

"Yes," she answered, "I just went through the list. He was with Elizabeth Carnaby. She's a big-time reporter from the Daily Herald."

This second blast from the past brought an instant reaction in McGowan's gut. Carnaby had written a series of articles which were meant to incriminate Fornesby at the time of Angie's death. "What in the world do they want now?" said Davis under his breath.

"Did you say something?" asked Connie.

"Just talking to myself. Rick Watkins called to make sure that we noticed that Slater had visited. Would you give Linda a heads-up about this? Watkins is worried that we won't do enough to reach out to them so we need to make sure that they receive a visit tonight when she organizes the calling teams." Linda was Davis' long-time associate pastor who supervised the congregation's evangelism activities. "Did they give an address?"

"Yes," said Connie, "they both listed a place on Homebrook Trail. They must be living together."

"Well, it's nothing that Linda can't handle. I will be tied up in youth club this evening."

"Literally?" said the secretary with a chuckle.

"Maybe," offered McGowan. "The kids get pretty serious when they decide to gang up on me. Anyway, Bill Slater and company will have to take back seat to forty elementary kids who want to outrun an old man playing freeze tag." They both laughed and went on to the day's work.

In the afternoon, Davis made the rounds to three hospitals. Most of the parishioners were scheduled for tests and elective surgery, but Becky Richards had been admitted to maternity. McGowan knew that she was only about six months along, and made his visit to her his first stop. Entering the room he sensed the emotional pain that hung over Becky and Chad who was seated at her beside and holding hands through the bed rail. Chad looked exhausted, and Becky's expression went beyond exhaustion. They stirred when they saw Davis.

"Dr. McGowan," they said in chorus.

"Becky, Chad, what's happening?"

Becky started to speak, but the words choked her. Chad provided the sounds that became monstrous words. "We lost the baby" was all he needed to say.

McGowan stepped closer to the pair and laid his hand on their joined hands. It was a gesture that took him back to the wedding two years earlier. Becky began to speak through her tears.

"They couldn't find a heartbeat, so they ran some tests and found that the baby was gone." Davis noticed the absence of the "d" word.

"I'm so sorry," he offered.

"The baby hadn't kicked for a while and we just thought he was going through an inactive period. My mom said that sort of thing happens, but when I went to see the doctor, well…," she broke off. Chad dabbed her cheek with a soggy tissue.

"They called me at work and sent us right over here," continued Chad. "They have induced labor so the baby will be born." Davis saw Becky wince and knew she was having a contraction. He waited until the tightness of her expression subsided. He nodded his understanding. The young couple would face labor and delivery together, but without hope of having a child.

"You said 'he'; was the baby a boy?"

"Yes," said Becky, "we were going to call him Joshua." The room went silent for a while, but it was a silence punctuated by another contraction.

"The nurse said that it will all happen very fast," said Chad. "This sounds terrible, but could you stay with Becky for a moment? I have to make a few phone calls and I know that they'll be coming to take us to the delivery room soon."

"I understand," said Davis looking to Becky who seemed to be saying that she did not want to be alone. "Sure." Chad left quickly. McGowan did not know whether it was the urgency of the task or he had reached his limit. He took Becky's hand at the bedside.

"This is about all that he can bear," she said after his leaving.

"This has to be tough on you both," he replied. A tightening of her hand told him that a contraction was beginning to well up. "Deep breaths," he coached as if being thrown back into the routine of the birth of his own children. The pressure on his hand relaxed.

"They asked me if I wanted to see him," she offered, "I mean, after the delivery. I don't know if I can stand that."

"What did you tell them?"

"I said that I didn't know. What do you think that I should do?"

Davis tried to think of all the articles that he had read on the topic of pastoral care and stillborns, but his intellect disserted him. What came out in his speech was a sense of the moment. "Whatever you do will be the right thing. If you'd like, I will hold Joshua."

"Thank you," she said, "for calling him Joshua," she added haltingly.

"That's the name you chose. That's what I will call him." A contraction came with total disregard for the moment. The door opened and Chad reappeared, followed by the nurse. McGowan stepped out to the hall while the nurse measured the dilation of the cervix. In a

159

few moments, Chad came to bring him back into the room.

"They're going to take us to the procedure room," he said. McGowan nodded.

"After the delivery, Dr. McGowan is to see the baby," said Becky to the nurse who glanced back at Davis. Davis nodded.

"I suspect that it'll be an hour or so," said the nurse.

"I'll be here," offered Davis.

For the next forty-five minutes, McGowan visited with a parishioner who was recovering from knee replacement surgery. Therapy was going well, and the man he visited was relieved that the pain of the surgery was less than what he had been enduring from his arthritic joint. He would be heading home the following morning. All through the visit, Davis' mind wandered back to the Richards and what they must have been experiencing. After twenty-two years as a pastor, he knew quite a lot about medical procedures and recovery time. He said goodbye to the surgical patient and tried to focus his thoughts toward what to expect when he arrived back at the Women's Center.

As he passed the nurses' station, he heard his name called.

"Dr. McGowan," said the nurse on duty, "I was told to watch for you. The procedure went smoothly and quickly. Mrs. Richards is back in her room."

"And the baby?" The nurse's facial expression told him that she wondered if he knew that the baby was going to be stillborn. He took away her confusion before she could answer. "I told Becky that I would hold the body, because she wasn't sure that she could bring herself to see him."

"Oh, I understand. Follow me, please." The nurse led McGowan through a door marked "Surgical Gowns Required, Staff Only". Before he could ask, she opened the door to a utility room not far down the corridor. "It's in here," she said. Davis saw a small bundle wrapped tightly in a blue and pink striped receiving blanket. Obviously someone on the staff had treated the event like a live birth, offering the stillborn the respect of a child, probably for the sake of his mother.

Davis took the bundle in his arms. The simple action brought back memories of his own children, now grown and in college, but Joshua would not be going home with his family, ever. He did not hold much stock in superstition about unborn souls, but he prayed for Chad and Becky. He spoke to the bundle. "Joshua, I'm sorry that you did not get to know them, they would have loved you very much." The stillborn looked like a perfect small doll. He set the bundle back in its place and went back into the corridor. He stood quietly for a moment, then retraced his steps to the public areas and back to Becky's room. His appearance brought expectant glances from Chad and Becky.

"I held Joshua and called him by name," he said.

Becky looked to Chad and then back to McGowan. "Was it awful?"

"He was beautiful," said Davis.

161

"Am I silly, Dr. McGowan, to want to see him?" Davis glanced at Chad.

"No, I wouldn't think that. I told you before that whatever you decided to do would be right. When couples lose a baby like you did, there's a tendency for everyone around to pretend that nothing happened. You two know differently, don't you?

"You felt Joshua inside, and that little kick made you both think about the future in another way. Now that he's gone, none of that will happen in quite the same way. You've lost a lot."

"We have," said Chad breaking his silent vigil. "When I called the office, it was clear that no one wanted to think about it. 'They're both still young,' someone said in the background. If I could have climbed through the phone, I would have…"

"There will be people who will understand," counseled McGowan. "Maybe in a few days we could all meet in the chapel for a private service."

"I'd like that," said Becky. "I think I'd like, no, I think I need to see him one time. Will you stay with us, Dr. McGowan?"

"Of course. I'll get the nurse." Davis quickly made his way to the nurses' station with the Richards' request. The nurse brought the small bundle to the room and placed the stillborn in its mother's arms. Chad moved closer and the two gingerly lifted the blanket veil from Joshua's face. Tears flowed freely from both as Davis looked on. When the emotions ebbed, he took the baby in his own arms. "No one can ever tell you that he wasn't real, can they?"

"No," said the two in unison.

Davis offered a prayer, and the three sat in silence for a long while until Becky said, "I've said my goodbye."

The nurse must have been standing nearby because she entered the room as if on cue. Becky kissed the lifeless form through the blanket. Before other words could be spoken, the bundle was carried off. In his own mind, Davis saw the utility room where he had first encountered the small body.

"Thank you so much for being here, Dr. McGowan," said Chad. As they walked to the door, he added, "I will call you tomorrow or the next day. I think Becky's parents are planning to come in and coming to the chapel would be good for us all." The two shook hands.

The image of the young family flooded Davis' mind as he headed south from the hospital. He had just enough time to get home and change his clothes before youth club. He was hardly in the mood for the craziness that he often instigated with the fifth grade crowd, but that was next on the schedule. He reflected on the fact that transitions were getting more and more difficult as he got older. Clearing his brain of one activity before engaging in the next was a challenge on this night.

No one was home when he arrived at his house. The message on the answering machine was from Rick Watkins, presumably before he had called the church office. Davis didn't listen. Trading his suit for a casual shirt and well-worn jeans was like escaping from a torture chamber. In any case, the kids would not get the best of him. In the fellowship hall, he amazed them, as usual, by managing to "freeze" every player in freeze tag. Try as they might, his feat was never achieved by one of the youth. He never shared his secret. While they could outrun him, they always tore around the room haphazardly tagging their friends. McGowan always kept an imaginary line between the "frozen" and the "thawed". Those trying to unfreeze their mates ended up like statues. In the kitchen he bantered with the adult advisors: "It's always good to score a victory for the old and crotchety!" By the time the running had stopped, the fifth graders were ready for a story and a craft. They all feasted on the traditional Monday night fare, hot dogs and chips.

It was not widely known that Davis spent his Monday nights at youth club. The church board had the idea that, as the pastor of a large congregation, he should be above playing games and telling stories. On the other hand, they lamented the fact that the high school students avoided Sunday services. McGowan could never get them to see the contradictions in their thinking. Why would young people sit through services where the worship leader was an unapproachable stranger? That evening Davis' streak remained unbroken. After his turn at being "it", the large hall was full of frozen statues; and then, the dinner bell rang.

It was just after nine a.m. the next morning when Connie Foster's voice came over the intercom saying that Rick Watkins was on the line. McGowan's stomach tightened in anticipation of the scolding he was about to receive.

"Davis, how did the visitation go last night?"

"I haven't seen the calling reports yet, Rick," he answered. "My guess is that the calls went well; we had a good team lined up." McGowan waited through the pause.

"You mean you didn't make the call personally? Davis, do you realize what it would mean if we latched on to Slater as a new member?"

"Rick, if he believes in what we're doing and feels comfortable here, he'll join. If not, well, he and I go back a long way and he knows me already. Meeting other members will be more of a draw for him than to talk to me, again."

"Oh, I didn't know that you were friends," responded Watkins. Davis didn't correct the misunderstanding of his comment. Slater and he were not friends. They had a brief encounter in front of a grand jury when McGowan had delivered the testimony that made a murder indictment evaporate in front of Prosecutor Slater's eyes.

"In the long run," offered Davis, "we need members who are committed to work with us rather than people who are impressed by a senior minister." The conversation soon wound down to a courteous exchange, but McGowan couldn't ignore the sinking feeling in the pit of his stomach. Why was Slater turning up in the pew? He knew that there was no love lost between them. The last thing he had heard of Slater was

165

a reported conversation when he had called Davis a "lying creep". As far as he knew, nothing had changed from that time.

When the associate pastor came into the office that morning, she brought with her the calling team reports from the evening before. Davis was impatient to find out what had happened.

"Linda," he said directing her to his office where he closed the door. "Rick Watkins is really pushing to know about Bill Slater. Did he get called on last night?"

"Actually, he wasn't home," she said, "but his fiancé was. That's the Elizabeth Carnaby who was with him on Sunday." Davis' surprised expression kept his colleague going. "They're evidently living together. She's very nice; it was a very pleasant visit."

"Were you there, then?"

"Yes. After what you said yesterday, I figured it might make some sense from a PR point of view."

"Thanks, that ought to take some pressure off," said McGowan. "Sounds odd to ask, but why are they here? Did they suddenly get religion?"

"No, it's less mysterious than that; they got engaged." Linda broke in to a brief chorus, "Goin' to the chapel, and we're gon-na get married..."

McGowan broke out in a laugh.

"My singing isn't that bad," she said with mock seriousness.

"No, it's not your singing. It's the idea of Bill Slater church-shopping, or, more likely, looking for a venue for a photo-op."

166

"He might be doing that," said Linda, "but I was impressed by Elizabeth. I know she's a reporter, but I think she's straightforward and sincere. She made no bones about it that Bill is going to make a run for the mayor's race and he wants tie up the loose ends."

"You mean, make her an honest woman?"

"Exactly. As I said, I liked her. She knows the score and doesn't seem to have much of a problem with it. Slater may have ulterior motives, but I think they genuinely love each other. Basically, he's dropped all the details in her lap. She's the one who suggested coming here to church."

"She did? Why?"

"She was very clear about that. It goes back to the interview she did with Barker Fornesby. Do you remember that?"

Davis nodded.

"She thought that he was a very decent sort of guy and knew that this was his church. She figured that he wouldn't suffer fools, and that you were his pastor back then, so you'd be okay."

"Bet she and Slater had a difference of opinion on that one."

"If they did, she didn't say, but they are really set on having the service here and having you officiate." Davis didn't know what to think, but the foreboding seemed to be gaining the upper hand over what some would claim to be a compliment.

"Do you think I can talk them out of it?" he bantered.

167

"I don't think so. She had it all worked out. A few weeks ago her secretary had called the church office to get the details. Connie told them that we didn't have the staff to perform outside weddings, so services in the sanctuary could only be booked for members."

"Good for her," said Davis, more to himself than Linda. He recalled all the years that he was held hostage to non-member weddings. With every weekend booked solid, he endured the surrender of the majority of his family time. Some of the board members felt it was a way to recruit new members. After keeping statistics for two years, he showed that all his efforts had led to exactly zero new memberships. To top it off, non-members viewed everything as fee-for-service, disrespected the staff and the building, and smuggled in enough champagne to set entire bridal parties on their collective ears. A members-only policy was finally set in place to protect the staff from the burdensome demands.

"Don't get your hopes up, Davis. They plan to attend the next new members' class." It was a sobering prospect for McGowan, but he would adjust. After the wedding, enthusiasms would undoubtedly cool. "I think it's not a bad thing," Linda continued. "She is going to leave the paper after the wedding and focus on charity work. I think she has an eye on being an active member. She's the sort that knows how to get things done, him too, for that matter."

"That's what I am afraid of," thought McGowan.

On Saturday morning a small group gathered in the chapel. More like a private meditation room, the quiet

168

space became a cozy retreat for Becky and Chad Richards and their parents. Davis had expected Becky's folks, but was pleasantly surprised when Chad's mother and father also came. They had been estranged for some time and went through a contentious divorce, but you could not tell on this day when they were forced to set aside their own egos. Linda, the associate pastor, was also there as were two familiar faces. When introductions were made, so were connections with the past. The two women had been attendants at the Richards' wedding two years earlier.

The service was more of a conversation. Linda and Davis read short passages, but mostly the families gave voice to both love and loss. In the end, they gathered in a circle of prayer. Both Davis and Linda thought it was a good beginning for the young couple to work through it, but they privately wondered if their part in it made much difference at all.

The next day, Slater and Carnaby were afforded the red carpet treatment. Rick Watkins apparently organized an unofficial greeting committee and hijacked the couple to the coffee time after church. It was a friendly gesture, even if contrived. Both Linda and Davis greeted them as they spoke with parishioners. The after-church gathering was often a time to pick up news of pending hospitalizations or important milestones. A granddaughter had been born to the Culvers and they were flying out to Seattle on Tuesday. Carolyn Watkins was back home and she and Davis moved to a quiet corner to debrief about her time with her niece and nephew and the flood of emotions that came from helping sort through her sister's home.

"Here's the man to ask, but I think you already know him," said Rick Watkins who had been hosting the visitors. With a wave Davis was ushered into a small pod which surrounded Bill Slater. "Bill has some questions about Presbyterianism," said Watkins, "you're the man to answer it." He paused and looked to Slater. A slight grin crossed his face.

"I was just saying," began Slater, "that I don't know where Presbyterians fit with other churches. I mean, do they have a lot of beliefs that are different from say, the Methodists?"

It was a standard question, one that would be covered in a new member's class, but all eyes were on McGowan, so it was not a time to smash expectations.

"We go into more detail in the membership classes," he began, "but the short answer is 'no'. In the past, there have been theological differences, but modern biblical scholarship crosses all denominational lines. What makes us distinctive is the way the church is organized as a representative democracy. The people elect elders to make the major decisions as a representative body, not as individuals with power. In fact, the word *presbyterian* comes from the Greek word meaning *elder*." He stopped speaking when he realized that he was actually boring himself with this standard answer.

Slater was listening intently. Davis couldn't determine whether he was that interested or waiting to drop the other shoe. When he paused, the shoe fell.

"So the familiar Bible teachings, like the Golden Rule and the Ten Commandments are all part of what you expect a person to believe?" Davis felt his face flush and inwardly cursed the involuntary response that had told Slater that he had hit the mark.

"Yes," he answered as matter-of-factly as possible. "The official teachings of the church honor most of the commonly held traditions."

"Being a lawyer, those moral codes really matter to me," said Slater with an innocent quality to his voice. "Imagine trying to find justice, for example, with witnesses that don't feel morally compelled to tell the truth."

"I don't think there's anyone here who wouldn't agree that justice is a worthy goal," countered McGowan. From his point of view, the conversation was over, but he did not want to turn away too sharply. "Excuse me," he said, "I need to thank the families that are serving as hosts. Can I get you more coffee, Bill?" The two had squared off in a game, and McGowan's own sense of justice wouldn't let him back down.

Slater turned down the coffee and Davis scanned the room. Beth was in a circle of women which included Elizabeth Carnaby. He walked over toward his wife.

"Davis, have you met Elizabeth yet?" she asked as he approached. In fact, he hadn't. The conversation on this side of the room was far less subversive than the one

McGowan had left. On the drive home, Beth could not stop talking about her new acquaintance.

"That Elizabeth is a hoot!" she said. "She's really funny, and smart. Her heart is in the right place, too. She said that after the wedding she's going to leave the paper. Bill thinks that her being there would be used by the other party when he runs for mayor. So anyway, she's looking for some sort of volunteer project. I told her about the adult literacy program, and she's interested in taking the training to be a tutor. Isn't that fantastic?" She didn't wait for Davis' answer. "She also thought that we might be able to get an article in the Neighborhood Section as well. That would be great publicity for the church."

"That would be good," offered Davis. His mind was creating a list of counterpunches to the left hook that Slater had landed. Some were academic, like: "The Golden Rule and Ten Commandments are terms entirely alien to the Bible. They are snippets of text that have been elevated to the disproportionate status of works unto themselves. Nowhere does the Bible tag Jesus' summary of the law as the golden anything; and nowhere does it refer to any special group called the Ten Commandments. The ten are a part of a much larger code to provide guidance for the covenant community." Such a defense would be academically correct, but suicidal outside a study group where the Bible was being read with sensitivity and openness. Most would string up a minister who spoke such an obvious truth. They would protect the idol of their list of ten by meting out punishments commensurate with their own particular brand of biblical ignorance.

Davis knew that Slater was not interested in the *Torah* or covenantal history. It was in his craw that Davis had lied before a grand jury. It was a case where justice would not have been served by the truth, and McGowan still believed that he had done the right thing. The truth about the death of Angela Fornesby was sworn to secrecy. He did not know Slater well enough to risk telling him that Angie's overdose of insulin was a simple mistake that took a life. He thought about Matt who was in college now. How would he handle the news that he had given his mother a lethal injection? He knew the answer to his own question; no one would be ready for that bombshell. The undisclosed truth was still the living protection of a young man. The truth was not something he would risk with Slater. If Bill saw only rules, he would never value the risk that Davis had taken in the jury room. If the contention between Slater and himself was to sharpen, the truth would not be one of his allies. If the charge against him was perjury, it was one that would stick.

The Carnaby-Slater wedding was being set up with very little lead time. It was his second marriage, but her first so they were attempting to find a not-so-fine line between low-keyed and societal blockbuster. McGowan knew that the headaches were just beginning when Connie told him that Channel 21 had called to say that they were sending a camera crew, and would that be any problem?

On the personal front, Davis drew a wide circle around Bill Slater. He could not help but notice, however, that the two newcomers had been quite regular in their Sunday attendance. The congregation seemed revived by their celebrity and the couple received more invitations that they could gracefully accept.

By the time they had been confirmed as new members, Elizabeth was already making quite a contribution to the life of the congregation. She and Beth had become fast friends. Beth, for her part, had introduced the reporter to the adult literacy program that the church had instituted to help both illiterate adults and foreign nationals who were pursuing the path to citizenship. In return, Elizabeth seemed to know everyone who was anyone in the Dayton country club set. For the first time in years, Beth felt that she had her hand on the pulse of what was happening and did not have to hear the news secondhand from her husband.

All in all, Davis was beginning to think that his fears were ungrounded. He knew that he and Slater would probably never be friends, but their truce had been defined and there was no reason why it should not hold.

By the wedding day, all the pieces had fallen in place. As Davis predicted, the rehearsal went well, and everyone knew exactly when and where the bride and groom were to be at any given moment.

Elizabeth's parents had died years earlier, so the honor of giving away the bride was given to Harold Jenks, the popular and retiring city mayor. He was a large African-American man who struck a handsome pose in his tux. He beamed like a proud father with Elizabeth on his arm as they got ready for the procession. Davis made his final pass through the narthex to make sure that the guests had been seated and the bridal party was lined up ready to go. With everything on schedule, he made his way through the corridor that ran beneath the sanctuary. He was breathing hard by the time he raced up the back stairwell to where the groom and best man were waiting.

"We should be ready to go when the organist finishes this final prelude," he said when he took his position near the front side entrance to the sanctuary.

"The church has been great to us," said Slater in a low voice. "Elizabeth is really happy here." The unsolicited comment stunned Davis.

"Like any congregation, we have our share of hassles," said McGowan, "but for the most part the people have a real commitment both to caring for each other and for making a difference in the world. I'm glad you are feeling settled here."

"My only concern is you," said Slater. "You did me harm when you threw that case four years ago. Just to let you know, I have a long memory, and, as they say, revenge is best when served cold. I think they're playing my song," he added. It was true, the music had changed and the first chords of the processional echoed through the narrow corridor.

Davis felt sick to his stomach.

"Come on, McGowan, the show must go on," said Slater, pulling at the door handle and literally shoving Davis forward toward the chancel steps.

Davis did as he had for decades. He closed off the emotional trauma and worked through the liturgy. He focused his homily on marriage and blessed the couple. At the close of the ceremony the couple kissed, the bride collected her bouquet, and the couple struck a pose on the edge of the chancel.

"Ladies and Gentlemen," Davis announced, "I am pleased to introduce to you William John and Elizabeth Grace, who are now husband and wife." Applause erupted and the organ blasted out a triumphant tune as the wedding party followed the couple in swift recession. Davis waited for the guests of honor to be escorted out of the sanctuary. When the groomsmen returned to dismiss the worshippers to the receiving line, McGowan took his leave, exiting through the side door of the chancel.

He found himself racing down the narrow hall to the small lavatory. He made it into the stall just in time to retch empty the contents of his gut. He stayed in this small tomb for five minutes seeking composure that came only as he consciously measured his breathing. He rinsed out his mouth and headed back to his office to change out of his clerical robes and back into his *civvies*.

He was sitting quietly in his chair when Beth found him.

"Everyone's headed to the country club for the reception," she said.

"Sure, okay," said McGowan trying to rally for the next scene in what had become a horrific charade.

During the car ride, Beth commented on the service. "You did an excellent service today, Honey. Everyone around me was impressed. The church was really packed. You really made it special, and you should be pleased."

Davis was deep in himself. Beth attributed it to the adrenalin letdown that often followed a big event. The parking lot at the country club was full, and McGowan had to park a fair distance from the clubhouse. He shifted the car into park and killed the engine. Beth had already unbuckled her seat belt and had opened her door.

"Beth, I don't want to go in there."

"You're just tired," she said, "but I know you, you'll brighten up as the party gets going."

"No, I won't," he answered, "not tonight. Slater as much as told me that he was going to get my job; and that's his goal in all this."

Beth stiffened. "Don't be like this, Davis. I don't know what has gotten into you, but you really have these people wrong. Bill and Elizabeth both told me that they are concerned for how hard you work and how much you have to bear. As far as I'm concerned these are some of the best people we know, and Elizabeth is becoming like a sister to me. You've got to stop being so paranoid. They're just trying to help you and you can't accept it. Grow up." She slid out through the

177

passenger side door. "Are you coming, or am I going in alone?" she asked.

Davis didn't move.

The author:

Rob Smith is an ordained minister who served in congregations for thirty-one years before accepting a position as a full-time instructor in Religion and Philosophy at Wright State University in Dayton, Ohio.

In 2005, he shifted his attention to his own literary efforts by completing several novels and creating a volume of poetry. In 2006, the Frost Foundation of Lawrence, Massachusetts awarded him the Robert Frost Poetry Award and *Night Voices* was published by Drinian Press.

He now resides on Ohio's north coast where he continues to write and works to restore a thirty year old British sloop. *Keelhouse*, the sequel to *Night Voices* is scheduled for release in 2008.

Rob holds a bachelor's degree from Westminster College in Pennsylvania and master and doctoral degrees from Princeton Theological Seminary.

Books from Drinian Press

Ohayo Haiku
by Nancy Brady

Ohayo is the Japanese word for "Good
morning." The poems in this book follow the
traditional form, but spring out of the Ohio
heartlands. Whether read as a morning
greeting or at some other time of day, they
are meant to inspire and soothe like a
greeting from an old friend.

ISBN 978-0-9785165-3-6

Night Voices
by Rob Smith

When an asteroid strike in Antarctica
throws the earth into volcanic winter, a
small group of sailors seeks refuge away
from the forces of destruction. Survival
depends on their leaving behind the
technologies of the twenty-first century
and reconnecting with the rhythms of
nature. Surrounded by calamity, these
families discover the strength of
community that is based on values that
extend beyond kinship

HC: ISBN 978-0-9785165-1-2
PB: ISBN 978-0-9785165-0-5

Order from your local bookstore or go to
www.DrinianPress.com
for links to online booksellers!

Printed in the United States
201680BV00002B/436-450/A